SONG OF THE BOATWOMAN

SONG OF THE BOATWOMAN

MEILING JIN

PEEPAL TREE

First published in Great Britain in 1996
Reprinted 2007
Peepal Tree Press Ltd
17 King's Avenue
Leeds LS6 1QS
England

ISBN 0 948833 86 6
ISBN 13: 9780948833861

 Peepal Tree gratefully acknowledges Arts Council support

CONTENTS

Victoria   7

The Tall Shadow   21

Song of the Boatwoman   31

Kin-sa: Second of a Pair   44

The Three-breasted Woman   52

Bear Woman   62

Perfect Secretarial College   71

Short Fuse   77

An Uneasy Life   86

Unravelling the Knots   93

Homecoming   101

Goodnight, Alice   109

This book is dedicated to Stella Kam, my mother, who collaborated on some of the stories and whose death at Easter 1996 leaves an eternally sad space in our lives.

Stella, star, you were a light in our lives
Your faith was an anchor in an uncertain world.
We loved you because you made us feel special.
Each one of us.

For everyone you met, you had a smile,
A kind word, some encouragement.
You were always ready to listen
And share a part of yourself.

From our earliest days we recall:
Going to church, going to Sunday school.
You wore a gold broach that said 'Mothers' Union'
And a locket that was a Bible around your neck.

'God bless you' was your favourite greeting,
Your favourite way of saying 'Goodbye',
And even if we didn't believe in God,
We felt blessed.

Stella, star, you were humble, generous,
Sometimes stubborn;
And with a wonderful sense of humour.
By your light we could always find our way home.

Stella, star, you will remain
That special light in our lives;
And as you make your journey home,
God bless, until we meet again.

VICTORIA

This story begin in Rose Hall, Berbice. A scream broke the night – cut it in two and wake up the neighbours to the fact that Victoria was in the world. What was a nice Chiney girl doing with a name like Victoria? It was still the days of the Empire, that is why. They call she Victoria, in honour of that fat English Queen that once ruled the waves. Victoria Wong-a-tim, born 1909.

Victoria grandfather, Ho A-yin, come over from China to work for Lainsi up at Kamuni creek. Lainsi pay the passage from China and, in return, they work for him in the charcoal pit. If any of the boys wanted to leave, Lainsi would kill them and throw them in the pit. All except Ho. He escape. He walk through the bush day and night, day and night, until he come to the Demerara. Then he tie a goobi round he head and jump in. Lot of Chiney men die like this trying to escape. Police used to see them and shoot. That is why you get the saying, a Chinee is a Chinee, just shoot any damn goobi. But not Ho. He defy Lainsi and the police, the bush and the Demerara. He arrive in Georgetown wet like a rat and with a hole in he behind from the gun shot. He went to work for Lee in the grocery shop and then moved down to New Amsterdam. That's where Victoria mother, Elizabeth, born. In turn, Elizabeth married a Chiney man by the name of Wong. Elizabeth was Wong second wife. The first wife, Elmina, did die in childbirth.

After Victoria was born, Elizabeth took in bad with malaria and she too died, leaving Wong with seven picknie: five from Elmina and two with Elizabeth. The family tree look like this:

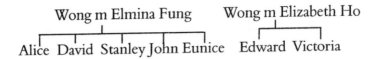

Wong m Elmina Fung   Wong m Elizabeth Ho

Alice David Stanley John Eunice   Edward Victoria

Victoria was the last of the seven: a small, stringy baby, full of fight and stubborn as a mule. Her big half-sister, Alice, had the caring of her. Vic was no easy child. Right from the start she would cry for her own way and later she did often fight with her brother, Eddie, bullying him into parting with his prize possessions: his fishing stick, catapult, and even his shoes one time.

When Victoria was 16, Alice got married to a Mister Chin. They moved away to Georgetown and opened a grocer shop, calling it Cho Chin. They took Victoria with them, putting her to work at the counter because she could handle people good good. She was a tall, slim girl with jet black hair tied back in two plaits. She liked the customers and the customers liked her. What's more, she had the knack for selling. If people came for a bar of soap, they often left with a pound of sugar or a loaf of bread. That was when bread was only penny a loaf or 8 cents a twist.

One day when Victoria was serving in the shop, Mr. Chin tried to rub his thing against her behind. Before that she had caught him looking at her, the horny old dog. Victoria was outraged. How dared he? Then she was ashamed. Take care it was something to do with her? What had she done to make Samuel Chin rub his thing on her behind? Worse of all, what if Alice found out? She felt shame burning up inside. She could not meet Samuel or Alice eye and kept following Alice around until Alice began to notice.

'Girl, what is the matter with you? You ain' eating, and every little thing you does jump. You see Ole Higue or something?'

Victoria flushed. She was the one that had wanted to come to Georgetown with Alice. How she was to explain she wanted to leave?

'Alice, I believe I going to go back to Daddy because I dream he last night, and he was aksing me to come back and help out in the shop.'

Alice looked hurt, she screw up her face and said, 'How you

8

mean, you dream Daddy? You mean you want to go back to Rose Hall. How we goin to manage without you, Vic?'

Victoria avoided to look at Alice big belly, otherwise she would have been tempted to stay. Alice looked worn out from caring for her six younger brothers and sisters and now she seem set to care for another six of her own. Victoria knew that childbirth was a dangerous thing. Alice own mammy had died from it.

'I suppose if you going to go, you will go, because you always pleased yourself even when you were a baby. I'll ask Samuel to take you to the train station on Friday,' Alice said.

Victoria bent her head in shame because she truly loved Alice.

The journey to Rose Hall took a whole day and when she turned up at the shop, Old Man Wong nearly had a fit because he think he seeing jumbie sitting on the verandah in the twilight.

'Eh eh! Is you! Wah you doing here gal?'

Victoria put down her grip and sat on the bench facing the old man. 'I come back because me ain' like it deh.'

Old Man Wong scratch his arm from habit. 'How you mean you ain' like it? You nah suppose to like it. You suppose to wuk!'

Victoria chin set in a stubborn way. 'I was wukking. But me ain' like it deh so I come back.'

'You ain' like it deh. All this talk about Georgetown this and Georgetown that. Girl, you too wara wara. How Alice goin to manage on she own?'

Victoria gazed down at the floor, while Old Man Wong continued to lash out with his tongue. Then all at once, like the rain in those parts, he stopped. Victoria, after all, was his youngest daughter, the last in the jar. She should have been a boy because she had all the fight her brother Edward lacked, a kind of wildness that sat well in a boy but spelled trouble in a girl, especially one like Victoria.

They sat in the dark listening to the mosquitoes, father and daughter.

'Ahwe better shut shop,' said Wong, at last. He got up slowly from his bench and stretched. He shuffled to the door and opened it. Then he turned to Victoria and said, 'Come an eat, or you gon stay out there all night?'

Meanwhile, life by the punt trench continued. On Fridays and Saturdays, Victoria would watch the cane-cutters breeze into the shop and spend they money freely. On Tuesday and Wednesday, she would listen to then asking for a little credit. They never asked her because they knew her too good. They waited until she was outside on the verandah, or inside at the back; then they asked Wong.

One Friday, instead of breezing into the shop, the cane-cutters came in grumbling and cussing: sugar price in Europe had gone down and Big Manager had cut they pay by sixpence. There was one big grumbling on the estate, you had only fo stand in the shop to hear it. Wong responded by giving more credit and hoping that things would improve. For some it did. Or at least, it got no worse.

Time passed slowly by the punt trench, it passed slowly on the inside from day to day, while on the outside, the years rushed past. From time to time, instead of a film at the picture house, there was a vaudeville show. Wong would change into his spare pants and they would walk up to Adelphi to see the amazing Sam Chase perform.

When Eunice got married, Victoria took over all the house-work and most of the ordering for the shop as well. Old Man Wong seemed happy to sit on the verandah and talk to Lallgee. They talked about the constitution, the price of sugar and the union. Occasionally, they would shout encouragement to the mule boy passing on the tow path, or gossip about the overseer and his missy.

World events passed them by until there came the time when the shop started to lose money. The sugar economy was deep in depression and Wong himself was too soft-hearted and allowed credit where he shouldn't have. Victoria didn't under-stand about depression but she understood credit.

'Daddy, we can't run this business if you keep giving credit.'

'How you mean credit? I only give credit to my regulars and they does always pay up,' answered the old man.

'But look how Singh owe you two and six and Ramchand four shilling.'

'They will pay up. Don't worry, gal.'

'How they goin to pay up? Douglas cut they money another six pence and Ramchand buss open he hand with a cutlass and all he can do is sit by the rum shop.'

'A man got to feed he family, Vic, you can't be too hard. Sugar gone down but it will go up again, you gon see.'

Victoria shook her head and muttered. She didn't know what they were going to do if the shop shut. She supposed they would go and live with David in Georgetown. She supposed. She liked David; it was his wife Esther that was trouble. Esther was a converted Christian and a converted 'lady' besides. She kept the house in Hatfield Street immaculate and insisted on saying grace and speaking English English.

Victoria thought of Stanley and Edward in Trinidad. Stanley had recently opened an ice cream parlour in Port of Spain and Edward had gone over to help him. If she had her way, she would open a parlour herself in Trinidad. She would work hard hard and she would make money.

Six months later, Wong sold the shop and arranged for them to move to Georgetown with David. Victoria took the whole business bad but Wong took it worse. He shuffle around the shop looking lost and refuse to let Victoria throw anything away, in case it came in for some use in Georgetown. On the day of their departure, when it was time to say goodbye to Laljee, Wong face sag in like an empty rice sack.

'Is forty years a bin here, ole fren, and now a going. I bin tink they goin to carry me out.'

Laljee laughed. 'Pun' trench glad to see the back of you, man.'

They patted each other on the back, hugged awkwardly and said goodbye. Change had finally caught up with them.

David owned a bakery in Georgetown with a house next door. He worked from five in the morning to ten at night everyday except Sunday when he went to church with Esther. Esther was pleased to welcome them in Hatfield Street. But neither Wong nor Victoria felt at home: the floor was too polished and the chairs too fine for a body to relax. Wong and Victoria avoided the house and threw themselves into working hard next door in the bakery. Wong insisted on getting up at five with David to help mix the dough in the big wooden trough. Esther tried to stop the old man from getting up so early and aggravating himself but he told her straight, 'I old but I ain' dead yet.'

Wong found it hard to adapt. As far as he was concerned, Georgetown was uncomfortable. It was hot. The sun seemed to bounce off the wood and bore right into his skin. Then there was the noise. There was a constant clatter from next door, people coming and going all the time. He complained off and on about the noise and ventured no further than the front step of the bakery or the hammock at the back of the house.

Then one day, what you think happen? Esther replaced Wong old cotton shirt for a brand new one and by doing that declared a kind of war. Wong in his entire life only owned two shirts at a time: one to wash and one to wear. They were both faded and soft and fitted him comfortably like skin.

He come in one morning, holding the new shirt and scratching his head, 'Vic, you see my ole shurt? Is whey me ole shurt stay? All I can fine is dis one.'

'Papa, is I remove your other shirt because it's worn under the armpit. I got you that new one from Bookers,' said Esther, smiling.

'Is why you thro way my good shurt for? I can' wear dis, he too hard.'

Esther sighed, as if she was trying to explain a difficult point to him. 'As soon as it's been washed a couple of times it will soften out. You will see. That other shirt was old. Think what people will say when they see you in that old shirt. They will think you're one of our employees, Papa.'

'Old! That shurt ain old. It good enough at Rose Hall. It good enough here. How you can sling out me shurt. You might as well sling me out. I older than the shurt!'

Esther laughed in a high-pitched, ladylike way. 'Papa! Honestly, I wanted to buy you something different. Progress is what they call it. The other shirt was very nice and so is this one. Let me wash it a couple of times and you will see.'

Old Wong shook his head. 'Gal, you head ain good. Throw way me shurt! I can' wear dis. An if you worry what you chuch frens tink, I goin to stay bottom house when they come roung.'

Esther shrugged and Wong stuck his heels in. Victoria sided with the old man, found the shirt passing for a floor cloth and rescued it for him. After that, life in Hatfield Street became difficult and each mattie found an excuse to stay out.

Victoria, for one, borrowed Esther's old bicycle and went down by the sea wall. Since Esther preferred to run the house by herself and the bakery got along without her, Victoria had more time than she knew what to do with. She felt lonely and a little lost. Sometimes, she went to see Alice in Leopold Street. The first time she went there she was shocked at how old Alice looked. Her hair was gray and her dress covered her frame like a dust cover over a piece of furniture.

'Eh eh, Alice man, let me comb your hair for you. And you must send these picknie over to Esther, let them see their granddaddy.'

Alice laughed and tossed back her hair. 'Send these over to Esther? And what gon happen to Esther furniture?'

Victoria smiled. 'Is true. Well at least send the big one.'

'No. The big one does help me with the others. Don't worry, Vic.'

'And where's Samuel?'

'He in the shop stocktaking.'

'Listen, Alice, I gat an idea to go to Trinidad to set up shop. Why you don't come with me?'

For the first time in years, Alice laughed with all of herself. 'Vic, you does get some ideas. How I goin to leave Samuel? I know he does have he eye on the girls but we understand each other. You now, you different. You young and stubborn with you own way And you mouth hot. But wait till you get marry, then you goin to see.'

Victoria shrugged. She wasn't going to marry and get like Alice. Not if she had anything to do with it.

Just before she left, Samuel appeared and Victoria received

her second shock that day: except for his hair receding a little, Samuel looked the same. She felt the old panic take over and was ashamed. She told herself it was over four years ago when Samuel had sneaked up behind her. But even now, she still could not stand to be near him. Victoria made an excuse to go, promising to call round as often as she could, but her mind told her she would not, could not, with Samuel around. Poor Alice. Well, she for one was never going to marry, or have six children. She brushed away an angry tear and cycled vigorously home.

Soon after the visit to Alice, Victoria struck up a friendship with the Lee girl opposite. The friendship was a big surprise all round because Nettie Lee was a Georgetown girl and had been to the Ursuline Convent School, in Church Street. From the way the two girls carried on they might have been bosom friends all their lives. In the evenings and on Sundays, they would cycle down to the sea wall and watch the boats anchored out at sea. Or they would sit in the hammock together and talk talk until the evening got black and the old kerosene lamp began to flicker. Esther welcomed the friendship because it meant that Vic was mixing with the right company.

'Nettie Lee is a good influence, Vic; even your Berbice talk is disappearing,' Esther remarked one day. Victoria pulled a face but kept her mouth in control. She was not going to let Esther vex her.

As it was a Sunday, Esther was busy preparing tea for her church friends. Victoria passed though the kitchen, scooped up a handful of genip and went down to fetch her bicycle. She had arranged to meet Nettie under the flamboyant tree and she was late. When she got to the tree, Nettie was already there.

'Your face is going to turn the milk sour,' Nettie remarked, when she saw her. Victoria replied by jumping on her bicycle and riding away, leaving Nettie to follow.

When they got to the sea wall they scrambled over, leaving their bikes on the road. By this time, Victoria was in a better mood. She watched Nettie roll out a mat and fix up an umbrella to protect her skin from the sun. The umbrella wasn't big enough to stand up in the sand so she had to hold it over her shoulder. It made her look awkward and out of place on the beach. Victoria resisted the temptation to poke fun at Nettie. Instead, she pulled out the genips from her pocket and put them on the mat. She bit into the green skin and sucked out the fruit. It was so sweet. She chewed on the seed to get out the last of the juice. As she chewed, she fixed her eye on the horizon. There was a ship heading out for the open sea.

'Look that boat there, Nettie, maybe it going to Trinidad.'

Nettie peered out at the horizon. Lately, she had stopped wearing her spectacles, which meant that she had to squint most of the time.

'It's the *Lady Nelson*, so more than likely it's going to Trinidad,' she said.

'You don't feel like jumping on it and going?'

Nettie shook her head. 'No.'

'Why not?'

Nettie shrugged.

Victoria threw the remains of the genip seed into the water. 'You think is joke I making about Trinidad?'

Nettie shook her head, 'No.'

'Why all you saying is no? What wrong with Trinidad, answer me that?'

Nettie laughed. 'Nothing's wrong with Trinidad, Vic. Look, if is a fight you want, why you come all the way out here?'

Victoria shrugged.

Nettie dug a hole in the sand and put a genip seed in it. 'You should go to Trinidad, Vic, you been talking about it long enough. Why you don't go and stay with your brothers?'

Victoria looked away; she didn't know what was stopping her, except that Trinidad was a long way from Georgetown, especially if she was to meet up with another Samuel Chin.

'If I didn't know you, Vic, I believe you too afraid to go,' Nettie said.

Victoria stared down at the sand, as if sand was suddenly interesting. She wiped the sweat from her face. Was Nettie right? Was that why she stayed in Georgetown? She was plain scared? She wondered whether to tell Nettie about Samuel Chin. Maybe Nettie would understand. On the other hand, Nettie was a well brought up young lady; she might feel it was

Victoria's fault. And to-besides, to tell Nettie was to shame her own sister, Alice. Victoria looked up. 'Me ain afraid to go, Nettie. When I ready I will go. Is the old man I studying. I ain wan leave he with Esther.'

Nettie nodded.

Victoria continued. 'What about you? Why you don't come with me when I go? We could open business together.'

'With what?'

'We could work in my brother ice cream parlour and make patties and pine tart. We could build up capital.'

Nettie shook her head. 'I don't like cooking.'

Victoria laughed. 'You don't have fo cook. I will cook. You got book learning and manners and English English. You can talk to them manager in department store and get dem to order from ahwe. Franchise you does call it.'

'I can't talk to them, without being introduced.'

Victoria glared at Nettie, 'I will introduce you.'

'And who will introduce you?'

'I will get somebody to introduce me.' Victoria shook her head, 'Girl, you are something else.'

Nettie adjusted her umbrella. 'Anyway, I prefer Georgetown.'

'Just when I get this thing settle you turn roung and prefer Georgetown!'

'What's wrong with Georgetown?'

'It got Esther in it.'

'Aside from Esther.'

Victoria drew a deep breath. 'Georgetown is small fry compare to Trini. We got to aim high. Trinidad ten times better than Georgetown.'

'I prefer Georgetown,' Nettie said.

Victoria shook her head in disgust. 'Girl, your head hard.'

'You're the one with the hard head, Vic.'

They stopped and stared at each other. Suddenly, both of them burst out laughing. It was too hot to fight.

Victoria got up and began to splash about in the sea. The sea was cool. She wiped the sweat from her face and tied her hair up in a knot. 'Come in nah!' she shouted. Nettie shook her head. Victoria scooped some water up and threw it at her.

Nettie shrieked and turned her head. Victoria played around some more. She liked the sea. It was different from the punt trench: wild and vast. It did something to a body, that and the breeze. She held up her arms in the air and opened her mouth in a silent shout. She was the sun and the sea and the breeze all rolled into one.

By the time she got back to Nettie, she was soaking wet. Her clothes clung to her skin, her feet were sticky with sand but she was happy. 'You shoulda come in, girl.'

Nettie shook her head. 'You look like a drown rat.'

Victoria grinned. 'The breeze will dry me off.'

'Your skin will get hard like leather.'

'Well, pass me over the umbrella, nah?'

Nettie laughed. She searched in her pocket and drew out a handkerchief. 'Here.'

Victoria took it and wiped her face and neck.

Nettie settled the umbrella on her shoulder. 'You know who I saw in Brick Dam yesterday?'

'Who?'

'Elmina Fung.'

'And?"

'She's engaged.' Nettie paused for effect. 'And she had a new hair style. Cut and perm.'

Victoria raised her eyebrows.

Nettie continued. 'I didn't know it was she at first. She look so modern. And you know what?'

'What?'

'I think we should have one too.'

It was Victoria's turn to laugh.

'Come on, I dare you,' Nettie said.

A week later , both Nettie and Victoria had their hair cut and permed at Nettie's house. The effect was to cause a storm with Esther.

'God gave you straight hair and you see fit to crinkle it up. It's nothing but vanity Progress is one thing but flaunting your hair like that and putting on lipstick is not fitting for a girl of your age. Or indeed, any age.'

'Lipstick? Is where you see lipstick, Esther?'

'I don't need to see. Now that your hair is permed you might as well paint your face and flaunt yourself in Bourda market. I declare, I'm sadly disappointed in you, Vic, and in Nettie, if it was she that persuaded you to have it done.'

'She didn't persuade me, Esther. Is the style now. Is modern and it suit me.'

Esther turned to Wong for support. 'Papa, I declare that Vic is getting wild. Staying out late and riding about on that bicycle all over.'

Wong shook his head, 'Don't look at me. Is you who calling for progress.'

Aside from the storm, the haircut had another unforeseen effect: it prompted a proposal of marriage from the Fong boy, who family owned the wholesale shop further down the street. Fong himself was a Home Chinee, that is to say, he came more recently and of his own free will from China.

Old Man Wong laughed at the proposal but, secretly, he was pleased because at last Victoria future would be settled and he could relax and die, or so he thought, only the blasted gal turn up she nose and said no.

Wong lashed out with his tongue, 'When you buy dutty chalico you gat to wear it til it tear. You don't listen to dis ole man. When coconut fall he can't fasten back. You goin to lef on the shelf.'

Victoria remained stubborn to the end. She didn't like the Fong boy because his face was hard. And although he was a Home Chinee, his ying-yang, ying-yang talk made her feel shame.

Wong shook his head and sighed; Vic had had her own way, but she would learn soon enough.

One Sunday, when Victoria returned from the sea wall with Nettie, she found the old man in a quarrelsome mood. Church visitors had invaded the house and he had retreated out the back under the verandah. For the first time in his life, he looked old and yellow, and he still had a cough from the cold he had caught staying too close to the brick oven.

'Vic, gal, please for make me a roti, a plain one. I can' eat that ting wah she call sandwich.' He shook his head and muttered, 'Tro way me shurt, I ask you.'

Victoria nodded in a kind of conspiracy and went to the kitchen to make the roti. She made a little sardine curry because it was the old man's favourite and hoped that the smell would not penetrate Esther's parlour.

When she got downstairs with the roti the old man lay asleep in his hammock, his hand lying limp by his side and a little spittle dribbling from his mouth. She went back with the roti and covered it with paper until the old man was to wake up. When he did wake up it was dark. He came upstairs, wolfed down the roti, and then sat in the Berbice chair looking out at the night. It was black. He could hear the crickets chirping. Old Man Wong lay back in the Berbice chair, sighed a deep sigh and passed way It was an easy death.

Victoria took the old man death hard, first blaming herself for refusing the Fong boy and then blaming Esther for trying to throw way he shirt. She wept secretly at night and hid the old man things in her drawer. She examined her life backwards and forwards: What was she going to do with the old man gone?

A fortnight after Wong bury, Victoria discovered that he had left what remained of the shop money to her. Victoria was stunned. The old man had cared enough to fix his will. Some of the old spirit returned. She recalled the story of grandfather Ho. How he had defied the Demerara and the bush. Could she do the same?

For the first time in weeks, she paid a call to Nettie Lee.

'Nettie, what you say about that business in Port of Spain. I get left the shop money Is not much, but is capital.' Victoria stopped when she saw Nettie's face.

'What happen to you?'

'Nothing, Vic, I'm pleased for you. It's what you wanted.'

'You staring like you see moongazer, girl.'

Nettie flush hot and stared pas' Victoria. Victoria opened her eyes big and started to mimic moongazer.

Nettie stamped her foot. 'Don't joke, Vic.'

Victoria stared at her. 'Is what make you so vex, girl?'

Nettie chin fix in a determined way. 'I can't come to Trinidad because I decided to get married.'

Victoria eyed her up and down. 'Who you marrying?'

'David Fong,' Nettie said flatly 'He asked Daddy and I said yes.' She stared nervously at Victoria. 'You don't mind, do you, Vic. You didn't want him did you?'

Victoria stared across the verandah at the street. 'Mind, Nettie?' She shook her head, absently.

Nettie patted her hair nervously, 'I never said I would go, Vic. Honest. I'm a Georgetown girl. This is where I belong.'

Victoria stared at Nettie. Nettie could not meet her gaze. She noted that the new hair style made Nettie's face look longer and older. She marvelled at how different they were, yet how quickly they had become friends.

Victoria recalled Old Man Wong, 'When coconut fall he can't stick back.' Nettie had chosen just like she had chosen and who was to say who was right?

'Have it your own way, hard head.' Vic said at last. She turned and walked quickly down the stairs.

Victoria took ship for Trinidad in 1934.

THE TALL SHADOW

He sent his shadow to court her. He waited until the day was far advanced, then stood in the sun so that his shadow would be at its longest. Raising his arms, he whispered, 'Ran-jai-pa', and sent his shadow scurrying.

Maralyn stood in the yard washing her feet, her blouse soaked through with sweat. She was tired from standing all day in the market selling roti. The fact that her basket was now empty gave her no satisfaction; she was tired and far too preoccupied. For one thing, taxi driver Winston, had asked her to the dance on Saturday night. And for another, today she had received a postcard from her cousin, Sandra. The postcard was a picture of a golden apple. It had the words, 'Greetings from the Big Apple', on it. Maralyn held the image of the apple in her mind like a forbidden fruit; one day, it was going to be her turn, one day soon.

'Maralyn, girl, come and help me mix the roti for tomorrow.' Her mother's voice cut through the daydreaming. Maralyn reached for the old cloth and dried her feet slowly. She would join her mother in the kitchen when she was ready. Washing her feet was a ritual she clung to, like washing away the aggravation and boredom of standing in the market. People wanted roti and more than roti when she stood there between the rum shop and the bakery. She thought about Winston again. Why had he asked her to the dance? She unhooked the mirror from the post and peered at herself: was there something different about her since she left that morning? Straight nose, flat forehead, high cheekbones stared back. That flat forehead and straight nose was the 'Buck in she', Moses had remarked on more than one occasion. Well, likely Moses was right. The 'Buck' in she had been the source of more than one joke at school. It was hurtful then, but now she didn't care; now her mixed ancestry had fulled out into features that were, beyond doubt, beautiful.

Maralyn smiled at the thought of Winston telling his passengers to wait in the car, while he calmly strolled over to invite her to the dance. She put the mirror back and turned to fetch water from the standpipe.

She saw the shadow when she reached the standpipe. At first she thought it was her own, but when she looked behind, she saw her own, and when she looked in front, the shadow, the other shadow, hovered as if it was waiting for her. Maralyn's heart skipped a beat. She threw the bucket on the ground and stepped backwards,

'Me na want nuttin to do with jumbie.'

The shadow approached her and, even as she backed away, it reached her because it was a tall shadow. Maralyn forgot.

She followed the shadow through the gate, across the ditch and down the road. The day's heat had lost some of its relentlessness and was giving way to a slightly cooler evening. Coconut trees shimmered in the late afternoon sun, but Maralyn was not aware of it. On she walked, past Teacher Thomas' house with the red flamboyant guarding the gate, past the baker shop, past the donkey in the field, the church; on and on. She may have heard the frogs croaking in the ditch, or the kiskadee in full song, and then possibly she did not, because all she knew was the shadow.

The house stood well back from the road surrounded by trees: coconut, mango and guava. It was large and you could tell it was well kept because someone had taken the trouble to paint it recently. One hand on the bannister, Maralyn climbed the stairs to the front door. She opened the door and went in without knocking. It was already evening. The jalousies were shut, to keep the shadows in.

At first she thought the gallery was empty, then she saw him hovering, like his shadow, by the jalousie, an old man, medium height, grey hair, large ears and a hooked nose. His skin was smooth and dark brown like old leather.

As his shadow returned to him, Maralyn remembered. Her eyes adjusted to the light and took in the gallery at a glance: polished wooden floor, rocking chair, Berbice chair, full length mirror, Chinese screen, long low table. Everything had an exactness about it, like the exact amount of furniture. There was no clutter, except perhaps the photographs, too many photographs.

Maralyn watched the old man warily, mindful of all the stories of jumbies and die-dies.

'Maralyn?' he said.

The sound of his voice made her jump. 'Who you is?' she said, hiding her fear.

He seemed to sink a little into the shadows. 'Sultan,' he replied. 'My name's Sultan.'

She grew bold. 'How you know my name?'

He walked out of the shadows towards her. 'I do because I've watched you. You're Moses' daughter. You sell roti in the market near the rum shop and clear fifteen dollars a day.'

Maralyn frowned over the fact that he knew she cleared fifteen dollars. She wondered if he knew she kept a dollar back when she handed the money over to her mother. She searched her memory to see where she could have come across this old East Indian man before, but her mind refused her the information. She decided to be bold, but eyed the door first, in case. It was good to be near the door.

'Is you bring me here?'

'Yes.'

'Why you bring me here?'

He spread his hands in a half-pleading, half-welcoming gesture. 'I wanted to meet you. A person can get a little lonely in a big house like this.'

Maralyn felt on familiar ground. 'You wanted to meet me, but what about me? I lef me mudder and the roti just lik tha'. Me mudder going to be vex.' She turned to go.

He raised his hand. 'Stay!'

Something in his voice made her pause, perhaps it was the urgency, or the ring of power in it. She hesitated. He was an educated man, and he had powerful magic. He crossed the room and switched on the light. The shadows disappeared. He rang a bell. It made a tinkling sound and brought a servant at once.

'Bring some refreshment, er, some sweet drink.' The servant disappeared.

'Sit down, won't you please,' he said, and as if to show her how, he sat down in the high-backed armchair.

Maralyn thought of her mother waiting for her to help with the roti: Eileen was a tall, strong woman, as tall as Moses. She would beat her if she didn't go home. Maralyn considered the old man: the old man looked frail, but he had powerful magic and he had servants. She hovered, undecided. She remembered the shadow and sat down, carefully, on the edge of the rocking chair.

As she did so she looked up accidentally and stared into the old man's eyes. Young eyes locked into old: he was the first to look away. She straightened her back in triumph. She had power too: youth was her power, youth and a recklessness in the face of... of what? What was she facing?

The servant returned with the sweet drink and offered it to her. She wondered idly whether it really was lemonade, or something else.

'It's only lemonade,' the old man said, apologising. Maralyn jumped, 'You does read thoughts!' she accused.

'No, no not really,' he lied.

She sipped the liquid carefully and, satisfied that it tasted like lemonade, drank it thirstily. She felt better afterwards and braver.

'So why you bring me here?'

Sultan clasped his hands together and leaned forward. 'I

brought you here because I need a companion. Someone to talk to. Share my pursuits. Spur me on to the finishing post. In short, I need a wife.'

Maralyn sat back, mouth open, staring. The old man was at least eighty. Old enough to be her grandfather. Great grandfather even.

'Me. You wife! Is joke you makin!'

'No. No joke. Perhaps you think me a foolish old man and perhaps you're right. No, let me finish. I'm old it's true. And weary. When you get to my age, all you have is time on your hands and all you think about is time... running out. I need a companion, someone who will spur me on to the finishing line.'

'Man, I don' even know who the damn hell you is?'

The old man smiled. 'Have you ever been to the County Court House in Campbell Street?'

'No. What I would be doin there? Is only crook and tief man does go there.'

'That's where you might have seen me.'

Maralyn sniffed. 'You never going to catch me in dey.'

The old man regarded her affectionately.

Maralyn stiffened. 'Any case, why me? Dey plenty other people in this damn place.'

The old man gestured, eloquently. 'You, because I've watched you. I like your stillness and your beauty.'

Maralyn drew back. The old ones were just like the young ones, maybe a little more humble but still after the same thing in the end. She started to rock backwards and forwards nervously.

'You can live here and enjoy my wealth. Have anything you like. I have more dollars than you can spend.'

'And what about the shadow. What about the shadow you send to fetch me?'

'A shadow is only a shadow.'

'But dis shadow do you biddin'. How I know I ain' endin up a shadow?'

'You have my word.'

'Pah! You word. You know magic and you got plenty wealth.

25

Where from I ask meself? Tek kay you got a baccoo working for you.'

The old man spread his hands wide and smiled. 'No it's all my own. All belonged to my family. My father was a lawyer, a very good lawyer. My mother owned land.'

He pointed to the photographs. Maralyn stared at them: they were old-fashioned pictures, framed exquisitely in gold or wood. Most of them were of East Indian people with intense expressions on their faces, as if the photographer had caught them by surprise. Maralyn shivered suddenly: the photographs made her skin creep. She looked away in the direction of the old man, keeping her eyes fixed on his chin so she would not, even by accident, look into his eyes.

The old man spread his hands in apology. 'You must excuse an old man's whim. I get a little lonely so I collect photographs of people.'

Maralyn shrugged. The old man shrank a little into his chair.

'Look I gotta go now, me mudder goin to kill me if I don't help she with de roti. Tanks for lettin me see de pictures. But I gotta go now.'

'Stay! I will reimburse your mother and escort you safely home.'

Maralyn wanted to laugh, escort her home, reimburse her mother. The old fellar was making joke.

'I could even help you get to the Big Apple.'

Maralyn paused, suspiciously. The old man had strong magic, of that she was sure. Otherwise, how he could say the only thing that she ever really wanted? The Big Apple. Sandra had done it. And so could she. She could lift herself out of this grinding poverty, this small, stinking world and go abroad.

'Yes, I could help you go abroad. Tomorrow, if you like. I have plenty money.'

She sat down carefully. 'Wha make you tink I wan go place?'

The old man smiled and sat back, his hands resting on the arms of the chair. 'I know you. I can see it in you. I know where you live. I know you share a room with your mother. Your clothes are draped over the clothes-stand because you have nowhere to hang them. The flies bother you, fetching water up and down bothers you, you bathe under the house and you can see through the floorboards because they're loose.'

Suddenly, Maralyn felt naked. She could see her poverty as a stranger might see it and she felt shamed. She sat silent, looking down at her hands.

The old man continued, 'The Big Apple is nothing, you know. A big city. Big buildings, too many cars, crime, poverty. People work their ass off in the shops, or worse, sell their tail on the street. You think the streets are paved with gold? No. Street paved with bodies, some dead, some alive. I could take you there, you know. They have a big hotel called the Plaza. You can ride to the top in a thing called an elevator, and see the whole of the city at your feet.'

Maralyn stared at the old man; her eyelashes, long and curling, drooped over her eyes. She looked like that other Maralyn, the blond one.

'There's a place I can take you to have afternoon tea, the Savoy. We can listen to music and enjoy a civilised life.'

She sat there looking at the gallery, listening to the old man talk about the Big Apple. In her mind's eye, she was there already, sipping tea from a china cup and wearing a dress made of pure silk.

'If you married me, we could travel; you would revive my interest in it all. We could see the wonders of the world, and at my age, that's all you want to see,' he added.

She eyed the old man. At your age you can't live much longer. She remembered the pyramids and the Taj Mahal, from her geography book at school. Was it true that those things existed somewhere? She could see herself escorting the old man there, as a guide or something. She stopped abruptly: the old man gave her the creeps. She guided her thoughts back to something safer. Eileen. Eileen was a harsh mother, but she loved her all the same. She thought that after she went to the Big Apple she would send for Eileen. And Moses? Chia! Moses can go hang heself! He and Eileen were always quarrelling. They quarrelled like a real married couple, to hear them. She recalled that lately the quarrelling had lost its sparkle and wondered whether Moses would go back to his wife in Rose

Hall. She felt sorry for Eileen. Eileen had struggled for the past twenty years to keep up the semblance of being married to Moses. As if the whole village didn't know he already had a wife. She, Maralyn, didn't care a hoot, although she herself was going to make damn sure she got a ring round her finger first.

The old man broke through her thoughts. 'You're wasted here, you know. You earn fifteen dollars a day, fourteen of which you give to your mother. How long will it take you to save up enough to go to the Big Apple? Three years? Maybe four?'

Maralyn thought of Winston. Winston was not bad looking. Tall and stocky. He earned good money driving a taxi. She wondered if Winston, like Moses, already had a wife and was just foolin around asking her to the dance.

She thought not. He had too much money in his pocket to have a wife.

'And if you marry Winston, worse. He'll want you to stop working and then you'll have children. You'll be stuck.'

Maralyn brought her mind round with a jolt. How did he know about Winston? Chia! This old man powerful.

She begins to be aware of the room, its stillness, the kerosene lamp, the rug brought back from his travels, the mirror, the photographs. Outside, it is dark, dark and still, except for the rustle of leaves and the crickets chirping.

She wonders how she will get home tonight and thinks of her mother again. Eileen, a powerful woman, part Indian, part African. Her mother will beat her if she doesn't return tonight, doesn't return tonight. She wonders where that thought came from.

'You could even send for your mother. There's nothing like family to make us happy,' said the old man, gesturing eloquently with his hands.

Chia! this old man inside and outside me mind. She tries to outstare him again but fails. She studies him instead. She notes how his skin sags and his clothes hang off him. He stoops a little at the shoulder. She imagines touching him and feels revolted. He looks sad.

Serve you right for readin me thoughts.

'Well, Sultan man, lemme tink about it. You know how things stay. I can't up and marry jus like tha'. I have to ask me mudder.' A wicked thought occurs to her. Why you don't marry me mudder and I come and stay with allyou?

The old man stretches his short thin legs. 'No.'

She looks at him and frowns.

'I mean no need to think.'

Maralyn laughs. 'How you mean no need? At least I have to go home and fetch me things.'

'Everything you need is here already.'

Maralyn begins to feel trapped. She remembers the dragon-flies she use to catch and tie with thread. She would let them fly a little and then tug them back when she felt like it. She often kept them in jars until they died. Maralyn rocks, nervously, in the armchair. It makes a creak, creaking noise. She has the feeling this is some sort of test, but has no idea what sort. Again, she remembers the string on the dragonfly: loose then tight, loose then tight and then always, always back into the jar. She looks at the old man's eyes. They look glassy. Her mind opens a little and she remembers where she has seen the old man. Why this fella used to be the old judge at the court house. Maralyn is shocked. She jumps from her chair and makes for the door; the door remains a long way away. Her legs feel like jub jub.

'Sit down, Maralyn!'

She sits down. Part of her thinks, the ole judge, fancy that. Then she panics.

'I goin home, ya hear me? I goin home.' She makes a mad dash for the door again and realises that it is the mirror. 'Gawd!' she squeaks. She crashes into the mirror and finds herself 'inside'. She knows she is 'inside' because she can see him on the other side. She hammers on the glass. She recalls the people in the photographs. Her mouth forms an Ohhhh.

The old man sighs, listlessly 'Why do they always try to escape?'

He thinks of the photograph he will frame that night, a beautiful photograph, a beautiful girl; she deserves the best, perhaps a velvet background and a ebony frame. He rings the bell absentmindedly. The servant appears.

The old man hangs his head. 'Only one for supper tonight and then I'll work on my picture.'

The servant nods.

SONG OF THE BOATWOMAN

In H– the Western Lake is beautiful and many tourists come every year to admire the scenery and inhale the fragrant breeze that wafts over the water. Boats ply to and fro to the islands, taking visitors to see the many temples and pavilions for which H– is famous. Poets come too to gaze at the lake and write verse about its beauty, or a beauty they have seen there, because H– is famous also for its pretty women.

It's difficult to appreciate such beauty when it's on your doorstep. Nonetheless, Zhe Hua and I often go to the lake to relax and amuse ourselves. Sometimes on Sunday she and I will spend the whole day on Three Moon island. We meet at a restaurant near the jetty and buy small stuffed buns which we carry over with us. Once on the island, we sit high on the rocks and devour the buns still warm from the cooking. From this spot we can see the dark green expanse of water, enjoy the peach trees and imagine that we are the only two people in the world.

Such were the happy times we spent together, Zhe Hua and I, until one day, when winter was almost done, my grandmother announced that it was time I married. I was not at all surprised by this announcement, because in the previous few weeks, Ah Po had gone out of her way to extol the virtue of marriage in the order of the universe. She had also hinted that the son of neighbour Zhao was a good reliable boy, that children were important, one child being better than none. Although I was not surprised by this turn of events, the announcement changed forever the quiet security of my life. My grandparents were not cruel people. In fact they were kindness itself, taking me from my village to live with them in H– so that I could earn a good wage and be a comfort to them in their old age.

The morning Ah Po spoke of marriage, I knew that the freedom I had enjoyed on moving to H– was coming to an end. I did not want to get married nor give up my independence, yet what could I do? My grandmother was only thinking of my future.

I went to work that day with a face as long as a strip of rice paper. I scarcely nodded to the other girls in my section and set to work immediately. Seated on the row next to Zhe Hua, I worked quickly, dipping my hands into the water and lifting out the white cocoons from which our factory makes its silk. The monotony of the work carried me along: the swish of the water as hands dipped into the tray and the click, clicking of machinery, as the threads were unravelled. Unable to stand my gloominess, Zhe Hua spoke.

'Xiao Huang, your face is as white as this cocoon. What troubles you, my friend?'

I started at the sound of her voice. 'Why nothing.'

'"Nothing" does not make you so quiet. Come, I know you too well, what is it?'

I continued lifting the white cocoons from the water, trying to consider what to tell Zhe Hua. I had known her now for four years, yet sometimes I felt there were things I could not tell her, for fear of ridicule. At last, I took courage from my friendship with her.

'Ah Po is arranging my marriage.'

Zhe Hua paused a second, hand in mid-air. 'And what about you, Xiao Huang. Do you want to marry?'

'No. I don't think so. But what else is there to do?'

Zhe Hua continued lifting the balls from the water and putting them in the tray in silence. She seemed to be choosing her words carefully.

'You could stay single,' she said.

I looked at her in surprise. 'What do you mean?'

Zhe Hua laughed. 'I'm not married, and neither is Jin Feng or Xiao Fu. We'll never marry.'

'Pah! That's what you think. Everyone gets married eventually, whether they like it or not, otherwise how do they have children, and who looks after them when they're old?'

Zhe Hua laughed again. 'You talk like your grandmother.'

'But it's true.'

'Such old-fashioned ideas. Listen, shall I tell you a secret, Xiao Huang?'

I glanced around to see if anyone was listening: heads were bent intently over the trays. All I could hear was the swish of the water and clicking of the thread.

'What secret is that?'

Zhe Hua leaned forward and lowered her voice. 'Me and some of the other girls, Jin Feng, Xiao Fu and Xi Ming have sworn a vow.'

'Oh? What vow is that?'

Zhe Hua smiled and brushed a stray hair away from her face. I could see a glint of amusement in her eyes.

'We've sworn never to marry,' she said.

The white cocoons slipped from my hands.

Zhe Hua began to giggle. 'Xiao Huang, you should see your face.'

'Huh! You should try to be serious when we're working, Zhe Hua.' I wiped my hands on my apron and began again.

'I am serious, little sister. Me and some of the other girls have sworn a sacred vow never to marry.'

'What do you mean?'

'Well, if one of us does, the others will drown themselves in the lake. We know other girls that have done it, I mean, sworn a vow and even some that have thrown themselves in the lake. We follow their example. After all, who wants to tie themselves to a husband like a dog to a fence, or an ox to the yoke. Our freedom belongs to us and so does our money.'

I looked at Zhe Hua with new respect: to swear a vow never to marry or die was the most exciting thing I had heard of. I had seen Tin Feng and Xiao Fu, walking hand-in-hand in the street, or sometimes at the cinema, giggling in the back seat. I had always envied them their independence. Now I knew their secret. What a discovery.

'But how do you do such a thing?' I asked.

'Simple. We stand in front of the shrine of the Kuan Yin on Three Moon island and we swear n...'

'Shh! It's Bai Lin.'

Silence fell as the section supervisor stood at the head of the work bench, a look of disapproval on her face. No one so much as dared to breathe. All that could be heard was the click clicking of machinery.

'Comrades, Monday morning there will be a meeting about factory discipline.' No one made any comment and, fortunately for us, the noontime bell rang. I got up from my stool and wiped my hands. My head was buzzing with ideas.

'Listen, tomorrow is Sunday. Let's go to Three Moon Island and I'll tell you more. If you want to swear the vow with us, then we will talk to your grandparents,' Zhe Hua said, at my side. I nodded my agreement.

For the rest of the day, I was cheerful and bright, thinking what a fine thing it was to have a bosom friend such as Zhe Hua, who would even be willing to talk to my grandparents.

On Sunday, my plan to spend the day with Zhe Hua on Three Moon island came to nothing because Ah Po arranged for us to pay a visit to neighbour Zhao. No doubt this was to be the preliminary to weeks of negotiation. I tried to wriggle out of the visit, pointing out that Neighbour Zhao knew me already since we lived in the same lane. But Ah Po insisted that things should be done properly. I wanted to tell her about Zhe Hua, and to let her know that perhaps I would not be marrying at all. I knew it was better for her to know now, rather than lose face later. But I lacked the courage to tell her since I had not spoken to Zhe Hua, and the vows of non-marrying were secret. Perhaps I should have told her, perhaps not. In any case, the visit went ahead.

It was a boring affair. I kept my feet still and my head down while Ah Po talked to neighbour Zhao about his health and the goings-on in the lane. Then towards the end, Zhao Qin, the son of neighbour Zhao, came in on the pretext of fetching his shoes. He was a thin-faced, serious boy whom I had seen often enough in the lane. We were formally introduced, much to our embarrassment, and then he left, without his shoes I noted. We stayed a little longer, discussing the problem of taking ginseng when one is unwell and then finally Ah Po nodded and we left.

Grandmother was well pleased with herself, pointing out what a good income we would have together and how lucky we were to have our own room once Mrs. Zhao cleared out the small room where she stored her pickles.

By this time it was already three o'clock and I was more than a little frustrated at having the visit to Three Moon island postponed. But just as I took off my shoes and coat, Zhe Hua arrived, insisting that it was not too late to go to the island. So I put on my coat once more and walked the short distance with her to the lake. When we got there, there were, indeed, plenty of people wanting to cross to the island as the weather was unusually fine and it was now soon to be Spring Festival.

We made the crossing with a family from Shanghai and when we got to the island, there was a spirit of festivity in the air. The shrines were crowded with visitors, so Zhe Hua and I went straight to the rocks away from the crowd. We sat down admiring the lake and the trees. Zhe Hua was in high spirits. All the way over, she had hummed a song and played with the children on the boat, whilst I had sat and brooded on the dark green waters. The visit that afternoon had depressed me. I saw myself married to Zhao Qin, living in the small room where the pickles were stored, becoming as serious as my husband, living a life of unbelievable sobriety and dullness. The future looked grim.

'Cheer up, Xiao Huang. Look, I bought you some melon seeds.' I took the packet of seeds and began to pick them open one by one.

'It's not the end of the world, you know. Girls like us don't have to marry,' said Zhe Hua, stretching her arms in the air.

I smiled fondly at her. If only I could be as optimistic as she.

We sat for some moments in silence enjoying the smell of the peach blossom. Voices of visitors could be heard chattering, and even someone reciting verse from the Soong poet, Lin He Qing.

'Isn't this moment beautiful, Xiao Huang? Don't you wish you were a poet and could capture it forever in your verse? Or a painter, instead of a poor factory girl. You know something? We are like this blossom: here for a short time and then we disappear.'

I sighed and sank deeper into my thoughts. 'Yes it's true. If only...'

'Think of the four years we've known each other, Xiao Huang. Think of all the things we said and did before arriving at this very spot.'

'Yes, how different my life was before I met you.'

Suddenly, Zhe Hua flung her arms around me in a rush of affection. 'Listen. I have an idea. Why don't we swear a vow now? To each other, binding our friendship together in this world and the next. I know some of the other girls have done it.'

I drew away from her. 'Seriously, Zhe Hua, is it true that you and the others have sworn never to marry? Will you really cast yourself in the lake if one of you marries?'

'Of course, it's true. We would rather drown ourselves in this lake than marry. Some of the other girls have even joined a sisterhood. They live freely in a house near Zhong Shan Park. And do you know something, Xiao Huang?' I looked, expectantly, at her.

Zhe Hua began to giggle. 'Old poker face, Bai Lan.'

'You mean our section head?'

'Yes, of course. She...' Zhe Hua lay back on the rocks and laughed with the sheer joy of being alive. 'She lives there too.'

I stared at her in astonishment. Then I too began to laugh at the thought of Bai Lan swearing anything as exciting as a vow. The laughter cleared the air and Zhe Hua began to talk excitedly about how she came to take her vow. The more Zhe Hua talked, the more animated she became, so much so she looked quite beautiful with her hair escaping in strands from her plait and her round face glowing pink with excitement.

And yet, strangely, the more excited she became, the more I shrunk at the thought of what I would say to Ah Po. Did I really want to swear eternal friendship with Zhe Hua? What

36

would the rest of my family think? What would happen if I changed my mind? Would Zhe Hua and all the other girls have to throw themselves in the lake? I shuddered at the thought. The more I thought about it the more silent I became, until at last Zhe Hua too ceased talking. I glanced at the sky: clouds had passed over the sun and everything looked dull.

'What's the matter, Xiao Huang?'

I started guiltily. Zhe Hua and I had always been close friends; it was impossible to hide my thoughts from her. And yet, how could I tell her that I was not ready to make such a vow. I was only twenty-two. What if I changed my mind? Zhe Hua had sworn never to marry; sooner tie a stone around her neck than a husband to her side. Yet she was willing to tie herself to me. Was I prepared for this? Was it not the same as marrying? And what about me? Did I feel the same? What would happen when we got older like Ah Po? Who would visit us? What about children? These thoughts and more raced through my mind as I stared into Zhe Hua's black eyes and she did not fail to see their imprint on my face.

She laughed in a false, high-pitched way. 'Perhaps you prefer the promise of a husband after all, Xiao Huang. Will that thin-faced little Zhao please you as much as me? Or is it the thought of his bed?' I reached for her hand but she pulled it away.

'Please, Zhe Hua, let me have time to think. I don't know if I want to drown myself in the lake.'

Zhe Hua drew back. 'No one will drown in the lake if everyone keeps to their vow.'

I stared at her. 'I mean in case.'

All at once the day seemed ended; the sun had set behind a cushion of cloud. Zhe Hua shook her self and gathered her things together.

'Think as much as you like, Xiao Huang, but don't be surprised if one morning you wake to find Zhao Qin tied around your neck like a stone. Your grandmother will have you married before you even know it. And as for me, perhaps I need to think too, whether I want to swear blood friendship with someone who is like a piece of wood on water, bobbing here and there. I too love to live, and fear the lake. You're the first I ever asked to swear a vow with me.'

'Please, Zhe Hua, I did not mean to offend you. I only need a little time to think. After all, an oath is an oath, whether I swear to Zhao Qin or to you.'

Zhe Hua leapt to her feet in a rage and started to walk away. 'Marry who ever you will. I don't care. But don't come running to me afterwards, little sister.'

I watched her leave. I wanted to call her back but I did not. Perhaps I was, after all, like a piece of wood on water? I sat watching the lake, wondering whether I would ever have the courage to throw myself in. I felt a terrible loneliness. I lay my head on my arms and listened to the wind touching the leaves. In the distance, I heard the sound of the boatmen calling as the darkness gathered around.

I fell asleep.

When I opened my eyes it was night. I leapt from my seat on the rocks, threw everything into my bag and scrambled down to the jetty as fast as I could. I knew it would be difficult to find a boat, for by now all the visitors would be gone. But perhaps if I knocked on the door of one of the cottages, I would find someone willing to row me over for a few extra fen. I stood on the landing for some minutes looking at the black waters of the lake. In spite of my predicament, it looked as beautiful as a piece of silk, shimmering in the moonlight. Years ago, as a country girl, I had learnt to love the blackness of the night because I could see the stars much better. I was not afraid. I gazed at the stars until my eyes began to water. All at once, from the surface of the lake I heard a song. It glided smoothly like a bird floating on a current of air. It hovered, soared and somehow, seemed to fill the lake with longing.

Dark are the waters,
Softly stirs the breeze;
Night, a longtime friend of mine,
Will you leave me too?

I stood bewitched by the song, for it captured my mood exactly:

loneliness, melancholy and a deep longing. I wondered whether it was perhaps a celestial being singing in the night. I began to be nervous. From the darkness, I saw a shape: a flat-bottomed boat such as were rowed by boatmen on the lake. As the boat approached, I felt a shiver of joy and dread: joy that it was a boat, and dread that the singer might be an immortal being. I stood uncertain on the edge.

As the boat approached the landing, I saw the singer, not a celestial being, but a common boatwoman. I was overcome with relief.

'Do you wish to cross back?' she asked.

'Yes, if you please. I fell asleep earlier and now there are no boats.'

She offered me her hand and I clambered in, clutching my bag. The night was clear and crisp. I was glad of the moonlight so that I could see, more clearly, my rescuer. Her face was oval in shape, her hair unpermed and cut short with a fringe. She looked like one of the female 'beauties' for which H- is famed, yet her face held strength and character that belonged more truly to beauty than prettiness. I studied her face in the moonlight as she rowed smoothly through the water.

It occurred to me, as I watched, that I had seen perhaps just a handful of boatwomen on the lake and those I knew mostly by sight. I had never seen this woman before.

'Tell me, have you been rowing on the lake a long time?' I asked.

'Long enough,' she replied.

'But I've not seen you before.'

'Nor I you.'

I lapsed into silence, wondering what to say next. 'Your arrival was most timely, otherwise I would still be stuck on the island.'

She nodded in reply. The silence was complete, except for the movement of the boat through the water. Yet I was determined to find out more about this boatwoman before the journey was ended, so I blurted out whatever came into my head.

'My name is Xiao Huang, I'm a silk worker from the

Number One District Factory. My mother used to be a teacher until she married my father. She wanted me to be a teacher too, but I knew I could earn more in the silk factory, so when my grandparents asked for one of us daughters to come to H–, I leapt at the chance and came.'

The boatwoman nodded. I looked down awkwardly at my hands. She clearly would not speak unless I prompted her directly.

'How about you, what's your name?'

'My name is Bright Jade.'

I felt myself shiver at the coolness in the breeze. The lake was chilly and full of magic.

'Tell me, what was the song you were singing just now?'

'An old song from a poet who lived by this lake.'

'He must have loved truly and known the lake well; his song is so melancholy.'

'Yes, I believe she loved it well. But when love and honour deserted, she threw herself in the lake.'

A boatwoman, a woman poet: curious. Had I not talked earlier with Zhe Hua of drowning in the lake? It seemed as if it was a common practice. All at once, I experienced a feeling of dread. How many women had given themselves up to the lake? What terrible secrets did it hold? How could it be, at the same time, a thing of beauty and terror? When love and honour deserted... I stared at the waters and trembled.

'Are you cold?' she asked.

'No. Not from the breeze,' I replied, grateful that at least she noticed me. 'I was remembering something I had said earlier.' Suddenly, the need to speak came over me. I looked at the boatwoman. I had never seen her before. I might never see her again.

'I speak to you as a stranger. Yet I know I can talk to you, perhaps because you are a stranger. Tell me, what would you do if you loved a person well enough and valued their friendship? Would you swear a vow of eternal friendship to please them? Or would you risk the friendship because you weren't sure? Not only this, what if your grandmother, who you love and respect and thinks only of your future, arranges for you a marriage, not a terrible marriage, an ordinary one, where you will not be mistreated, and who knows, may be even loved, what would you do?'

I looked at the boatwoman. Over her shoulder I could see the landing of the town getting closer. I wanted her opinion, desperately I wanted her to cease rowing and answer me. I wanted the crossing to carry on for longer.

She stilled the oar in response. 'Friendship is a precious thing. Do you love your friend?'

I thought about Zhe Hua. Did I love her? Not like a woman loves a man. Then as a woman loves a woman? I closed my mind around the thought. What if she was a man? Would I swear to her? I did not love Zhao Qin, yet why did I feel compelled to marry? Was it out of love for my grandmother? Or was it simply because everyone got married? What about Zhe Hua, she wasn't married. Did I love Zhe Hua, or was I doing it simply because I didn't want to marry Zhao Qin? Could one love a woman, the same as a man? My head began to reel.

Finally, the boatwoman spoke. 'What if your grandmother had arranged for you to marry your friend. Would you have married her?'

'That is not a real question. Girls don't marry each other.'

'But if they did and your grandmother arranged it, would you have done it?'

'Yes.'

'Then think of your vow as the same thing.'

Suddenly, Bright Jade looked sad. 'Yes, there is only the lake. And forever is long enough.'

'Somehow, I feel as if I'm doing what everyone else wants me to do, not what I want to do.'

'What do you want to do?'

I thought for a long time. I was so unsure. All I wanted was to carry on as before: working in the factory, having money to spend and going to the island with Zhe Hua. Did I want anything else? I thought of the house in Zhong Shan lane, of Bai Lan, the section supervisor, living there. Then I thought of the small room where Mrs. Zhao kept her pickles. What should I do?

'Perhaps I would like to try the house in Zhong Shan Lane but without the thought of drowning in the lake.'

Bright Jade laughed a curious bitter laugh. 'The lake is not a terrible place. I live here all the time.'

'I don't mean living, I mean drowning.'

For a moment I felt a chill on my spine at the thought of drowning. What an unlucky thought. I crossed my fingers.

Bright Jade continued. 'You do well not to vow hastily. Perhaps that is what the vow is for: to prevent us from being hasty; after all, friendship is a precious thing, worthy of such a solemn vow. If your friend is serious, I am sure she will wait.'

At that moment I looked at Bright Jade, the moon cast a silver sheen on her face. I thought she might be the most beautiful woman I had ever seen. She took up her rowing again and as the boat neared the landing I felt a terrible sense of loss. I shook myself. Perhaps it was the lake.

'Do you row here all the time?'

She smiled for the first time. 'I row the lake all the time.'

'Then if I came down tomorrow evening, would you be here?

'Perhaps here, perhaps on the lake.'

'Would you be here if I brought Zhe Hua?'

'I am always on the lake.'

I could get no promise from her. I felt compelled to sit in the boat and talk on into the night. Yet already we were at the landing and it was time to get out. I began to search for my purse to pay her, thinking that I would give her everything there was in it. As I found my purse, I tried one last time to discover the identity of my boatwoman.

'Where do you live? Perhaps I could visit you?'

'I live on the lake.'

I dropped the purse and all its contents on the floor. 'How stupid of me,' I stammered, reaching down to find the coins. I was trembling from head to toe. From emotion or from cold, I knew not. As I scrambled to scoop up the coins, behold, to my utter terror, I saw that Bright Jade had no feet. I sprang up from my seat nearly capsizing us both. I would have fallen between the landing and the boat had it not been for Bright Jade who held the boat steady with her oar. I began to pant with fear. Should I scream or be sick?

Bright Jade smiled with such sweetness, I felt my terror subside.

'Farewell, Xiao Huang,' she said.

I backed away, trembling with fear, yet how I longed truly to embrace her. I stood swaying on the edge of the landing trying to catch the last snatches of her song.

Dark are the waters,
Softly stirs the breeze;
Night, a longtime friend of mine,
Will you leave me too?

I wanted to be sick. I had spent the crossing with a ghost. The woman poet who had jumped in the lake? I shivered. She threw herself in the lake when love and honour deserted her. Had she sworn a vow too? I stared at the waters until the last echo of her song could be heard no more. Then I wept.

At last, I turned from the lake to the streets. They seemed warm and crowded with families strolling or eating outside. I glanced at my watch. It was only eight o'clock. Someone stopped and asked for directions. I pointed them the right way. I thought of Zhe Hua with longing. Truly, she would be the only one I could tell.

'Xiao Huang!'

I spun round in the direction of the voice.

'Xiao Huang. There you are. I was worried. When your grandmother said you hadn't returned I came to look for you.'

Zhe Hua. I stood and hugged her as if she might suddenly disappear.

'What is this. Why do you hug me?'

'Zhe Hua, I'm so happy to see you and I have a lot to say. Come, let us walk by the coffee shop and I will tell you.'

KIN-SA: SECOND OF A PAIR

My sister and I clung to each other in my mother's womb until, on a long contraction, I was forced out into the world. My sister tried to hold onto my foot, but on that long contraction she let go, preferring to remain in the warmth of the womb rather than join me in a hostile world.

Eventually, however, she too was forced out, head first, and we lay there stunned and then shrieking as loudly as we could. Even at that early age, I did what I was always to do: before I opened my mouth to scream, I waited for her to join me in a chorus. People called us twins and, indeed, we were very much alike at the beginning.

A month after our birth, when it seemed sure that we would stay, a naming ceremony was held to honour us. The priest held me high and pronounced the name my father had chosen. 'She will be Kin-oi, being born first of a pair.'

In turn, my sister was blessed and named Kin-sa, meaning the second one of a pair. Upon being named Kin-sa, my sister screamed in a sort of rage, so that the priest who was holding the mare's milk, spilled the remains of it on the floor; a most unlucky sign but for my mother's quick action: she mopped up the milk and threw some salt to placate the spirits.

From the beginning we were viewed with some confusion and a little fear because we were twins, not a common occurrence among our people. However, my father had much power so they forgot their mistrust and grew to accept us.

My father was a wealthy man. He owned a herd of sheep and goats, six camels and seventeen horses. He was also the chief of his clan so people came to him to solve their disputes. As I was the first born, being older than my sister by five minutes, I would inherit the herd and the grazing rights and, if my father had his way, even his place as head of the clan. Such was the custom in our tribe.

From the age of three, my sister and I shared a secret: she could speak to me without anyone knowing by simply popping into my head. Had I been older, I might have been unnerved by her intrusion into my thoughts, but we were young and I thought it was normal. By the time we were older I had gotten used to it and, besides, I knew we had a special relationship because we were twins.

As we grew, it became apparent that we were not exact replicas of each other: she and I were different, as far as it is possible for two peas from the same pod to be different. In both looks and temperament we differed. My face was rounder than hers and my eyes were a dark shade of brown. She, on the other hand, stood an inch taller and her eyes were a deep violet colour. However, from the back we were indistinguishable, having the same shock of black hair and the same build.

Aside from this, she was prone to sudden bursts of rage, while I was a very placid child. Where she led, I followed, always giving way to her demands and often taking the blame for her misdeeds.

At the age of nine, things began to change subtly in our home. It started on the day of the choosing ceremony when children's horoscopes are cast and a craft is chosen for them. On that day my sister was given a sword and I was given a pipe: she would learnt to fight and I would learn to speak and reason.

I was, at the time, bitterly disappointed because I had wanted to wield the sword, to ride at the head of a raiding party and do great acts of daring. But it was not to be, for it was the wishes of my family and the choice of the astrologer.

Later that day, I threw away the pipe by the stream where the animals drank. It lay discarded like an empty milk skin. I did not want to be a leader with words, nor liked for my fair judgements. I wanted to be a warrior like my sister.

When I returned to the tent, my mother knew what I had done.

'Go and fetch the pipe, my daughter, or we will not be able to turn the flow of your father's displeasure.'

I ran straight away to the stream and searched wildly in the dark, but the pipe was gone. I grew afraid and thought that I might run away, but there was nowhere in all the Steppes I could go and besides, how would I survive?

My father discovered the loss the next day, when he called me to bring the pipe so that he could explain the markings.

'I have lost the pipe,' I whispered, as I stood before his gaze.

'Then find it,' he said coldly and turned his back on me.

We searched the stream in turns, my mother, my sister, and I, but we never found it. So I was whipped and made to sit at the entrance of the tent.

'You cannot value what you have, so now you must do without. If you do not want to lead the clan then better for us your sister should lead,' said my father.

After that, our lives took a serious turn. Where before, we played childish games riding and hunting, now we learnt all the skills of survival on the Steppes. We learnt to lay traps, to separate one horse from a grazing herd and shoot arrows while riding at full speed.

On top of this, when Kin-sa went to learn the sword with my uncle, I sat and copied out letters like a scribe. Sometimes, during this task I would become distracted because Kin-sa, wishing to share with me her lessons, talked in my head all the time she wielded her sword.

One day, my longing to try the sword was so intense my sister sensed it.

Let us trade places, she said, in my head.

'How do we dare?' I replied.

We will dress alike and no one will notice, least of all our uncle. Besides, they will not imagine that we dare.

'He will notice that we do not fight alike.'

He will not notice among so many.

That afternoon, when I stood and faced my uncle, he looked straight past me. Had I cowered, perhaps, he might have noticed, but I did not. I moved as I knew my sister moved and no one noticed. In this way we managed to learn both fighting and writing, although I wonder that people did not notice how differently we worked from day to day

At the age of thirteen, my father began to make Kin-sa and I sit in the tent where all discussion was held; he wanted us to see how disputes were settled and problems solved. Normally, it would only have been me he made attend in the tent, but because of the pipe, he was going to let us both have our chance at leading. In this way, he sought to punish me, little thinking that I found this by far the better arrangement.

So we grew together, and in most things my sister continued to lead. It was she who decided who we would be friends with, and who we would hate; what we would be good at, and in what we would fail. It was not that I lacked a will of my own. It was more to do with the circumstance of our birth and her need to be foremost.

For my part, I felt sorry for anyone who my sister happened to hate because her hatred, like her temper, had no limit. One day our cousin Jelmei, older than us by two years, sought to make fun of her as we practised with our bow. We were trying to shoot at targets and when she missed he threw a dead hare where the arrow should have gone.

'A remarkable shot!' he cried, at which everyone laughed.

'A remarkable dolt!' I shouted, furiously.

My sister remained silent and went to retrieve her arrow.

That night, as we lay on the k'ang, she spoke in my head, Jelmei needs a lesson.

'What do you mean to do?'

I will show you tomorrow

The next day, she bid me dress my hair like hers and wear her tunic. We took our bows and when we found that Jelmei had gone to see to his father's herd, we followed him up the hillside.

There he is, she spoke in my head. You will approach him from the front and I will take him by the side.

When he saw me, he nodded. 'Still shooting arrows,' he called.

'Yes.' I pointed to his side, 'And there is a hare beside you.'

He turned quickly to look and as he did so, my sister shot him in the arm. I will not forget the look on his face. He did not trouble us again.

47

As we grew older, there began to grow between my sister and I a kind of rivalry: we both wanted to excel in horse-riding and we both had dreams of winning the annual horse-racing competition at the Spring Festival. Each year we tried our luck galloping our horses over the race course. But never did we cross the line first. At the age of fourteen, because it was the last time we would be permitted to enter, we practised more fiercely than ever; my sister because she wanted to be first and prove to my father that she was a good leader, and me because of the glory.

On the day of the horse-racing contest in our fourteenth year, we led our mounts to the starting line. As we sat waiting for the hush, I looked along the line and knew that we had a good chance of winning because my father had mounted us on two of the finest horses.

Good luck to you, Kin-sa said in my head.

I turned and bowed to her, 'And to you, my sister.'

At the drop of the flag we were off, racing like the wind over the muddy Steppes. Full of that feeling of exhilaration that only horse-racing can give you, I urged my horse on. Yah! Yah! We led all the way, from the first hill to the last and as we approached the finishing line, I turned to look at my sister. As I did, she crossed the line before me. She was jubilant. And strangely enough, so was I.

About three weeks after the Spring Festival, a strange rider appeared in our midst. He sat with my father in the tent and then left straight after.

Later, as we sat at our meal, my father announced, 'I have received a good proposal.'

'From whom?' my mother asked.

'From Karbul of the Shang-gor tribe, for Kin-sa.'

My mother smiled. 'He must have seen her win at the Spring Festival.'

'But father, I'm not ready to marry and move so far away,' said Kin-sa.

'Nonsense, you are fourteen and more than ready. Your husband will be a chief one day and you will have a place of importance,' my father replied.

'But was I not given a sword? Should I not at least prove I can use it?'

'And prove it you will, because they graze on the border and there are plenty of horse-thieves and bandits there.'

My sister hung her head in defeat. But not for long: she looked up and flung one last plea. 'But did you not say that I might lead this clan some day?'

My father hesitated. His eyes shifted to my face. Then to the face of my sister. The silence in the tent was heavy.

At last he spoke. 'He asked for the one who crossed the line first at the horse race. And besides, a clan cannot have two heads. Much as I would like you to stay, in this matter we will follow the custom. She who was first born will lead.'

From then on my sister became quiet and thoughtful. She did her chores and continued her lessons. She even came to the tent of discussion. But I knew she was not satisfied and would not rest until she was.

One evening I was lying on the k'ang waiting for sleep, when suddenly, she spoke in my mind.

Sister, I have a plan to steal some horses.

I sat up in the k'ang and stared at her wide eyed. 'Horses!'

Yes. We can travel as far as the border between Udor and B'Ngal where the Bator tribe capture wild horses. We can steal some of their horses and return in three days.

'It's madness.'

No. Some of our people are going on a raid to Udor in any case. They wish to enlarge their herd and strengthen the breed.

'We don't need more horses.'

We do. It will be my dowry

'We will not be allowed to go.'

We will not tell them.

I turned over in the k'ang and fell asleep.

We left before dawn the day after, taking with us a blanket and as much food as we could steal. I was excited at the prospect of our adventure, for the vastness of the Steppes seemed to beckon as we rode North towards the mountains.

On the third day we reached the mountains. We climbed the

ridge and saw a small camp of the Bator; they breed their horses wild then capture them and train them to the saddle. The camp was small: only two tents and an enclosure with nine horses.

On the Steppes, it is customary to raid at dawn, so at least the victims have the whole day to pursue. But we were young and impatient and decided to raid at dusk.

Because there are only two of us, reasoned my sister.

As soon as the light began to leave the sky we positioned ourselves on the ridge. There was no one about, except for two or three men relaxing around the fire. We kicked our horses forward and rode down to the enclosure. Opening the gate, we herded all the horses out so they would not have mounts to pursue us. There was much shouting and waving but we raced off like the wind leading the horses between us.

But someone must have had a mount because, suddenly, we were being pursued. We galloped at full speed and, as I turned in my saddle, I saw our pursuer drawing a bow.

I will shoot her, or she may catch us, said Kin-sa.

She took an arrow and fixed it to the bow. She wheeled her horse around, waited for the pursuer to come within range, and shot. Perhaps she hit her, perhaps she did not; in any case, we did not pause to look, neither did I slow our pace. On and on we rode, long after the sound of pursuit had died.

Eventually, when the horses could no longer gallop, we slowed to a trot. I turned in my saddle and felt a searing pain as my sister slumped forward and clung to her horse's mane.

'Aye sister!' I shouted. I rode back and caught her as she slid from her horse. I helped her down to some rocks nearby and left the horses to roam where they would. For what use were they to us, anyway? I took off my coat and wrapped it around her, my mind numb with shock. I could hardly bear to look at the arrow coming from her side.

'Don't worry. I will get help. You will be fine,' I whispered.

Yes. I will be fine, she repeated in my head. Then she grinned, We did it my sister.

I nodded. 'Yes, we did it.'

I took off my shirt and tried to staunch the flow of blood. I could scarcely steady my hands.

At last she whispered, 'No use. I'm dying.'

Out here on the Steppes we are used to death, but this I could not accept. I held her against me, not daring to move because of the arrow. Her eyes closed in pain. As the night progressed, she grew restless. And then agitated.

'What is it? What do you want?' I asked.

She fumbled in her pockets.

'Let me get it?'

She shook her head. Exhausted, she drew from her tunic my pipe: the one I had so carelessly thrown away by the stream five years ago.

'Look. I hid it,' she said, simply

I gazed at her face, so like my own, trying to retain each memory we shared right from the womb. My wild foolish sister, you only held on to my foot because you wanted to be first, always first. And would that you had been, for how will I live without you now?

I held her in my arms as if trying to detain her. But her spirit lifted, hovered, and then left me.

THE THREE-BREASTED WOMAN

My lover is a woman with three breasts. I only discovered this after I got to know her well and slept with her. She and I met by accident at a meeting to talk about increasing production targets. I was struck by how easy it was to talk to her, as she had a way of listening that made you think she was genuinely interested in what you had to say.

After the meeting we went to my house and carried on talking well into the early hours of the morning, until it was time to get ready for work. That was how I met Venus, or Blue Orchid, as she later became known. Blue Orchid was, and is, a remarkable woman. Even in this world where we are like so many pebbles on a vast beach, she is the pebble that glints when the sun catches it.

But getting back to Blue Orchid's breasts, three in total: they stand out from her naked body like soft, smooth, undulating hills, and each hill is topped by a firm, dark nipple. Not many women have three breasts, but the ones who do are special. They inherited the third breast from a particular set of people who long ago settled among us. In those dim echoes of the past when we were ruled by women, we hunted mainly, but farmed on a small scale as well. We made clay pots with 'primitive' designs which you can see in museums. Some of the designs are of fish, others of four-legged animals. In the times of the Ba Po we would sit by the stream when the work was done and pick the lice out of each other's hair, long hair which we braided to keep out of the way. In those days, the three-breasted women were honoured because they could look into the future and tell us what fortune might bestow on us.

Throughout the ravages of time, and in spite of the invasion and conquest by alien men, Blue Orchid and women like her, have kept their power. They do not disclose it to men or even to some women. Men do not know about this third breast, or if they do, they do not know how or why we have it. They think it is something to do with our intuition.

Along with the power to see into the future, women such as Blue Orchid have the power to influence certain events. That is to say, they have the power to curse. They may not use this power for their own ends because that would make them next to gods. However, they may use it to dispense justice.

I remember the first time I saw this power at work. It was about six months after I got to know Blue Orchid and it happened at work. There was a party to celebrate the end of the old year as well as the breaking of our original production target. There was a good deal of drinking and merrymaking as people relaxed and talked to each other. One person who enjoyed herself was Mei Quan, an older woman, who, for various reasons hardly went out or kept company. The works' party went on late and Mei Quan stayed drinking and talking. It was the first time she had enjoyed herself so much. One of the people she chatted happily to was Mr. Hu, the production manager. Mei Quan basked in the attention she got from this man, who was normally somewhat aloof. At the end of the party he offered to escort her home. There was nothing unusual about this as Manager Hu lived in the same direction as Mei Quan, and she was relieved not to have to walk home by herself. That was the end of the episode, goodbye old year, welcome the new. We did not realise anything was wrong until the third day of the new year: Mei Quan was absent from work two days and this was very unusual for her. However, we supposed there was a good reason for this and only decided to call round in order to collect the master key for all the lockers which Mei Quan was responsible for.

When Blue Orchid and I arrived at Mei Quan's house we found her at home. She looked the same as usual except for her eyes: they were dull and red as if all the sparkle had been knocked out of her. She explained that she had been unable to sleep for two days now, and this was why she had not been to work. I was very sympathetic as I knew the agony and distress that occurs when your brain churns over and sleep refuses to come. I happily accepted the explanation, but Blue Orchid continued to probe Mei Quan until she burst into tears and started sobbing fit to break anyone's heart. Then she told us the story of what had happened three nights before.

'I was enjoying myself, mind; I don't get out much and it was like being a human being again – people were talking to me. I admit I had too much to drink, too much for me that is. But it was a party and when he stood talking to me I felt I was worth something. When he offered to escort me home, I didn't think twice. He's a married man, a senior manager. When we got to my house, he asked for a cup of coffee and I thought, why not, I won't disturb the girl because she's away. He came in and we had a cup of coffee and...' At this point Mei Quan burst into tears. For to cut a long story short, Manager Hu had raped her.

When we heard this we were so shocked we couldn't say a thing (well, what can you say?). I was for confronting him straight away. Death by hanging would have been far too kind.

'He should be strung up!' I insisted.

However, Blue Orchid restrained me and pointed out that we had to consider Mei Quan's feelings. I was suddenly filled with the deepest sense of shame and rage on her behalf. But this was nothing compared to the profound shame and guilt that Mei Quan felt in allowing herself to be escorted home and have this thing happen to her, as if it was her fault.

'You can't blame yourself for inviting him in,' I insisted. But all my words could not banish the feelings of disgust and shame she felt towards herself. It started in her face, which she kept hiding, and seeped right down into her vagina, which she saw as her most dirty part.

'I'm 54, with two grown children. You'd think I'd know better by now,' she kept saying.

I for one, felt terrible; for I too had a grown daughter and would I have known any better? Indeed, what was there to know? Manager Hu was a 'respectable man'.

Mei Quan made us promise, against our better judgement, not to tell anyone, not even her daughter who was arriving back that evening.

'We still have to do something about Manager Hu,' I insisted. But Mei Quan stubbornly refused.

'Let be,' said Blue Orchid eventually.

At that moment there was a knock on the door; a piece of paper flew through the letter-box. We peered through the window and saw Manager Hu making his way down the stairs. We watched in silent rage. Slowly, Mei Quan picked up the paper: it was a note inquiring after her health and asking why she hadn't been to work. He told her to report as soon as possible. We were all filled with the most complete rage, and Manager Hu would surely have been pulp by the end of it.

Blue Orchid and I spent the rest of the evening with Mei Quan and only left when her daughter arrived home.

On the way home we walked in silence. The few street lights cast eerie shadows and made everything seem threatening and sinister. I tried not to think of Mei Quan and Manager Hu but somehow I kept seeing her struggling with him in her own home. Unable to stand the silence or keep the thought from my mind I turned to Blue Orchid and said, 'The man should be exposed directly.'

'True. But exposing him may mean exposing Mei Quan and we must consider that,' she said.

'We can't leave him to rape others,' I said. Then another, more terrible thought, came to my mind. 'What if he's already raped others?'

'That too,' said Blue Orchid.

I stayed with her that night as I had no wish to walk to my unit alone.

The next morning when I got up, I saw Blue Orchid in deep meditation, the light from the early dawn giving her ebony skin a strange blue tinge; such is the spiritual beauty of the three-breasted women. I did not question her afterwards as I knew she had found a way.

A day later, we were working in the machine room when we

heard a scream so loud and terrifying that everyone froze in silence. Working in the wood factory we learn to live with such screams but this was more terrifying than I had ever heard. We rushed out to the main floor to see a crowd of people gathered around the circular saw. I was puzzled because we had never had an accident there before. Nothing prepared me for the sight before us. It was the body of a man. Someone had hastily covered him with a blanket but his torso was angled badly and blood had seeped through and stained the blanket dark red. 'Manager Hu,' someone whispered.

Apparently, he had fallen against the belt of the saw and been neatly sliced in two. I was shocked.

'Workers, kindly report to your section, after which the whole factory will close for the rest of the day,' came an announcement. I turned to look for Blue Orchid, but she was nowhere in sight. Then I recalled the curse and the power of the three-breasted woman. I trembled violently. Was it the curse or was it an accident?

I went to look for Blue Orchid. She was changing by the lockers. Her face was set in a grim way so I asked her no questions.

Curse or accident, it seemed a terrible death, but when I recall Mei Quan's face and her broken spirit, it seemed as if a kind of justice had occurred.

★   ★   ★   ★

I am called Venus or Blue Orchid. My real name is unknown to all but a few. That is because a name is a thing of power and not given lightly. I am descended from a line of women known as the ones with three breasts. We are sages. We live to perhaps six hundred years old. I am one hundred and thirty five years old by your reckoning although I look no older than twenty five. That is because seven of your years is one of mine.

When I first met Morning I liked her straight away. I felt as if I had known her before, perhaps in another life. I knew, too, that she and I would become lovers. It is not unusual for one with three breasts to take a lover. We are constant and our friendships last at least a lifetime by your reckoning. The only thing we must accept in taking a lover not like ourselves is that they will grow old, while we remain still young. I knew this when I became lovers with Morning. She was already fifty-one when I met her – a baby by our standards but full grown in yours. I liked Morning from the beginning because she had an alertness about her that was uncommon. She could see and analyse things quicker than most, and was not afraid to speak her mind. This gave her a reputation for hot temper and belligerence which in all the time I knew her was not true. For the rest, I believe she was of ordinary beauty, big-boned, large hands, fine brown eyes and close-cut black hair. When I met her she had just moved into a smaller unit because her son had married and moved North.

After the death of Manager Hu, Morning became more interested in the workings of the 'curse' and the history of my people. She thought, like most people, that the 'curse' was a matter of ill-wishing. This is not the case at all. It would be more accurate to say that we have the power to construct mirrors. When a person is forced to look into the mirror they see only the sum of their actions (or inactions). This often leads them to despair or change beyond the 'normal'. In the case of Manager Hu, what I did was exactly this: forced him to look into my mirror, which was enough to send him toppling off balance. I did not expect him to die as he did. This is beyond my power. Nonetheless, die he did, and I and my clan are responsible. We hold in our custody this power and this responsibility. We cannot shape it to our own interest, only apply it according to its own laws.

Morning had always assumed that she was older than I and had often used this to end arguments between us. On this occasion, we were moving into our unit and she was carrying a box of food up the two flights of stairs. At the top of the stairs she stopped for a rest. Then she drew a deep breath and carried the box to the kitchen table, collapsing on a chair beside it.

'When my son left and I had to move,' she panted, noisily, 'I thought it was the last time. Now here I am again. This is most definitely the last time. I'm getting too old.'

I followed close behind her carrying the last and the most heavy of the boxes. I put the box on the table and stood gasping for breath too.

'Morning, you make so much of your age, but I am far older than you.'

She looked at me, laughter already in her eyes.

'What do you mean, you're older than me?'

'I am older than you because I am one hundred and thirty-five years old and you're only fifty-one,' I said.

She shook her head. 'You're a baby, not much older than my son.'

Something in my look must have held her because she suddenly became serious.

She gazed at me intently. 'It's impossible.'

I sat beside her at the table. 'We of my clan age differently to you. The history you speak of is not so long ago for us.'

'How old do you live to then?'

'Perhaps six hundred years. It is part of our heritage. Like the power to mirror.'

She remained thoughtful.

'And will you ever age?'

'Not in the same way as you. For the most part, it is difficult to tell our age without listening to an account of our journey. I am considered young in my clan.'

Morning shook her head and laughed. 'Then at fifty-one, I am the baby in this partnership!'

I nodded.

Morning got up from her chair and started to unpack the box she had carried up the stairs. I could tell from her expression that she struggled with the idea of my age and what it would mean to our friendship.

'You are older than I but look no older than my son or daughter. This is hard enough. When I am seventy, you will still look no older than now. When I am dead and long gone you will, where will you be? Here with another lover, now perhaps still in kindergarten?'

I lowered my head for I could see she spoke in anger.

'Perhaps you should take a lover from your own kind,' she said.

58

'Perhaps. But none of my kind are here. And besides, the heart does not often follow the head. Why can we not enjoy what we have now?'

She shrugged. 'Is it only the women or the men too that live to this age?'

'The males of our tribe live to a great age but not as long as the women. It has something to do with the third breast and the power to mirror.'

'What else should I know about your lineage?'

'For the most part we are like other women. Our feelings and responses are the same. If we fall like Manager Hu, we will die. If we do not eat, we starve.'

'Yet living to such an age makes a difference.'

'True. We are slow to become angry. We see life patterns much better. Our memories are important, so we are trained to weave them like a carpet and call them up when necessary. This has given us a reputation for being able to see into the past. Aside from this, we are constant and loyal, we never...'

'Stop! Perhaps a little at a time would be better. It's enough to know you are different.'

From then on our partnership became more easy and my age, or rather her age, ceased to worry her. We lived happily in our three rooms, going to work at the factory, spending time at home or going for long treks in the woodlands. Moreover, because of my reputation for settling arguments, our home became a focus for many women. Some came to seek a settlement, others simply to visit. One regular visitor was Mei Quan who, since the death of Manager Hu, had regained some of her sparkle and had even begun to play a role in factory life.

One day, perhaps a year after we had moved, there came another dark-skinned woman from my clan. She was known as Kenensat. She had travelled a great distance from the North, bringing news of my kinfolk. I welcomed her with great enthusiasm, hugging her and holding her hand all the time.

'Fifty years since last I saw you. And you're a baby still, Venus,' she said in her deep, sonorous voice.

'And what of you? The last time I saw you was at my

mother's house. You came to bid us farewell before your journey to the Delta.'

'And what a journey!'

'When did you return?'

'Three years ago.'

'What news?'

She shook her head. 'It will be a month in the telling.'

I led her to the kitchen where Morning had prepared a banquet to feed us.

'And my mother?'

'Very well. She sends her greetings. Your brother is ageing rapidly but he manages well. Your sister has a daughter and is preparing for a journey.'

'Eat!' Morning commanded.

We ate with relish, enjoying each morsel, staring at each other, laughing and jesting.

When all was cleared away, we made Kenensat a bed and she fell asleep straight away, exhausted from her journey.

Much later in bed, Morning asked me about my kin and why they had chosen to settle in the North.

'We of my clan are great travellers, our life span is long so we journey and settle where we will. We learn the customs and language of our hosts and adapt ourselves to them easily. My grandmother came from the Upper Delta, the great cradle of civilisation more than two continents from here. She chose to settle in the North because the climate was suited to her needs. That is where my mother was born – in the arm of a mountain. And I too. I have never seen the Upper Delta and like many who have settled here over hundreds of years, I rely on the memories of others, fed on news brought by one such as Kenensat. Eventually, we who have never seen the Delta, make the journey, some settle there but most return.'

Some weeks after the arrival of Kenensat, there grew in me the desire to see my kinfolk, especially my sister before she made her journey. Stronger still, yet deeply hidden was the desire to see the Delta too. I became restless. When Kenensat spoke in passing of some small thing she had seen there, I listened raptly. I began to stare into space and started going for long walks alone in the forest.

None of this escaped Morning. 'Blue Orchid, I have never seen you so restless. Is it time for you to journey?'

I turned to stare at her. 'No.'

'What then?'

'I wish to visit my kin in the North.'

We stared at each other, the knowledge of our difference, passing between us. If I started on a journey to my kinfolk and then a journey to the Upper Delta, I would not return in her life span.

I gazed at the grey around her temples; it made her black hair seem darker still.

'I wish only to visit my kin – a journey of not more than half a year.'

She bowed her head in agreement.

A week later, I resigned from the factory and prepared to leave for the North with Kenensat. Many of my friends came to see me, bringing small gifts for the journey. I was moved by their thoughtfulness.

On the eve of my departure, Morning handed me a quilt made of fine silk. I put it together with my small bag.

'A small bag for such a long journey,' she said. I embraced her. 'Most likely I will be back by Winter.'

She nodded.

That night we slept not at all, and when the dawn came, I took my leave.

BEAR WOMAN

Makepeace rolls over and switches the radio on.

'Police are still looking for the robbers. That's the end of the news. AA Roadwatch, 12.32. A burst water-main near Blackfriars Bridge is causing delay to south bound traffic.'

'That's all I need. A burst water-main at Blackfriars Bridge.' She switches the radio off and contemplates getting out of bed. If she gets up now she can have breakfast outside before going to work. She continues to lie where she is, a vague feeling of fatigue overcoming her muscles, making it impossible for her to move. She hopes that the fatigue is from working-out and not from the flu that is going about at the moment.

She stares at the ceiling and thinks about training. Last night she had trained at the dojo and her teacher, a young Japanese man, had told her she wasn't ready to take her black belt. After all the practising, the push-ups, the evening jogging. She bit her lip in disappointment. She knew she was clumsy. Her teacher had told her so at the beginning. She envied his grace, the ease with which he moved. She imagined that Samurai were like that. She imagines herself a Samurai, moving with grace and speed. Like a butterfly, her grandmother would have said. Hastily she blocks out her grandmother's voice; it has a nasty habit of surfacing, like the old lady herself.

A loud knock on the door compels her to wake. She contemplates ignoring it, pretending she's not at home. The kids on the estate have taken to knocking on her door and running away. They pick her, instinctively, because she lives by herself and looks foreign. Not as foreign as if she wore a sari, or a salwar, but dark-skinned nonetheless. The knock turns into a kind of pounding that sends her pulses racing. Instinctively, she knows that whatever it is, is unpleasant. She allows fatigue to take over momentarily, then pulls herself together. She hasn't been training at the dojo everyday for nothing. She yanks herself out of bed, pulls on her clothes and stumbles downstairs. Whoever it is is going to get the full force of her anger.

She opens the door without pausing to check who it is. In her current mood, she is more dangerous than any would-be attacker.

'Makepeace, I'm sorry, only I didn't know what to do...' She stands staring at her neighbour, Odette, a small attractive woman in her early twenties. Odette looks distressed. She is flanked by a gaunt, desperate-looking man.

'Odette, what on earth...'

The words hover in the air then vanish: Odette is propelled forward across the threshold. The reason for her distress becomes apparent immediately to Makepeace: the man has a revolver.

'I'm sorry, Makepeace, they stopped me on the staircase when I went to empty the bin...'

The man points his revolver at Odette. 'One more trick like that and I'll blow your head off.'

He turns his gaze to Makepeace, and indicates with his gun that she should lead the way up. Makepeace looks at Odette. Odette opens her mouth to apologise but shuts it again like a goldfish.

Makepeace turns and leads the way upstairs. All fatigue has disappeared to be replaced by a dull ache in her forehead and an overwhelming fear for her life. The man will probably shoot them both if he doesn't get what he wants.

She leads the way to the sitting room, hesitating at the sight of the mess: furniture pushed back, a curtain hanging off the rail, piles of books, magazines and comics on the floor. For some reason, she feels ashamed of the mess. Grandmother would certainly have had something to say about it.

'You'll have to excuse the mess...'

The man pushes past her and goes straight to the window.

Without turning his back on them, he peers cautiously out. The flat is on the topmost floor of the block and commands a good view of the courtyard below. Satisfied that there is no sign of pursuit, he turns his attention to Odette and Makepeace.

'Sit!' he says.

The women obey.

Makepeace takes her courage into her hands and asks, 'Is this a hold up?' Her voice squeaks so much she can barely recognise it.

So much for the grace and speed of a Samurai.

The revolver man chooses to ignore her.

She opens her mouth to ask another question, but changes her mind. The revolver man has a cruel look that precludes any reason, much less pity.

She glances at Odette. Odette is holding herself rigid, her lip trembling slightly. Serves you right, thinks Makepeace. Why on earth were you emptying the bin, and what the hell were you thinking of bringing him here? Odette feels her resentment and a look of apology crosses her face. Makepeace relents. Odette knows about her brown belt. She mistakenly believes that Makepeace can, somehow, deal with guns and thugs. Makepeace frowns. She wishes that she did not feel so inadequate.

Her gaze shifts around the room and lights on a wall poster of a bear. She had bought that poster because her grandmother had told her that she was guarded by the spirit of a bear, a brown bear, *Ursus Arctos*. Perhaps that explained why she was so clumsy. On the other hand, Grandmother had said a lot of strange things, in a language barely understood by Makepeace; she could hardly be relied on for anything as ordinary as an explanation.

A sudden sharp rap at the door sends her pulses racing. Her heart skips a beat and starts to pound anxiously. She looks at Odette. Odette looks trapped. Makepeace fears the worst.

'Open it!' says the revolver man.

She stares at him in surprise, gets up awkwardly from the sofa and lumbers down to the front door. She draws a deep breath and opens it. A young man in a leather jacket stands on the step.

'Let him in!' says the revolver man from the top of the stairs. She lets the newcomer in: a man with sullen eyes and quick nervous movements. He makes her feel more on edge than the revolver man. She follows him up the stairs.

'Did you get it?' says the revolver man.

The newcomer shakes his head.

The revolver man mutters an oath.

'It's not my fault...'

Makepeace stands awkwardly before them. The revolver man waves her into the sitting room before continuing.

'Anything else?'

'Nothing.'

'We'll have to wait it out.'

'And get holed up in this place?'

'Suit yourself. We have to split in any case.'

Makepeace stands near the door listening intently; her fate and Odette's is being decided at that moment in the corridor.

'I told him it was wired. The fucking cunt didn't believe me.'

She stops listening and tries to remember what she had heard on the radio that morning about a bank robbery. Try as she might, she can only recall the burst water-main. The most important things first, she thinks, bitterly.

She sends another wave of pure resentment at Odette for the invasion. This time, Odette has the grace to blush. If only she had buried her head in her pillow that morning, Odette would have had to go elsewhere. Or even be blasted to bits. Hastily, she thrusts the thought aside, feeling ashamed of her mean-spiritedness. She and Odette are neighbours, friends even.

'Go on then, piss off!'

'O.K., you're the boss, you always have been. This evening then.'

Makepeace stops listening, and moves like lightning to the sofa. In her haste, she trips and falls into it. Odette's expression hovers between laughter and deep dismay. The newcomer appears at the door, and all laughter dies out. The women compose themselves: Makepeace pulling her shoulders back, Odette crossing her legs. The newcomer stares dismissively at them and throws himself into the nearest chair. The revolver man follows at a leisurely pace. He positions himself near the window so he can see out. Silence.

Makepeace stares cautiously from one man to the other. One is blond and red-cheeked, volatile; the other is pale, gaunt, with nerves like steel. Between them they will kill us, she thinks. Quickly she blocks out the thought. Another thought creeps in. It curls around her conscious mind and settles there. Hostages. She stares at the revolver man. He is the one who will decide what happens, because the newcomer, the younger one, depends on him somehow.

She wonders whether she should have done something right from the beginning. Perhaps if she were a black belt instead of a brown belt, she might have been able to think of something. She wonders what her instructor would have done in the circumstance: a quick blow to the temple and death. Once again she is reminded of her failure the night before. She recalls her teacher saying, 'You must learn to focus your energy better. Perhaps you should try wrestling.'

She swallows her disappointment. A cow gives milk, a nightingale sings, and a giraffe eats leaves. The law of the universe, according to Grandmother. Suddenly the telephone rings, shattering the silence. All eyes turn to the revolver man. The revolver man has his finger on the trigger. Makepeace breaks into rapid speech.

'It's probably my workplace. I should be at work now.'

The phone continues ringing.

'I'm supposed to take a group of pensioners to...' The revolver man aims his gun at the phone. Makepeace ducks instinctively.

This is it, Makey. Ahhhhhhh!

The ringing stops. The revolver man relaxes his grip on the gun. Makepeace tries to compose herself. She sits on her hands to stop them from shaking. We'll both be killed. I know it.

She glances nervously around. No one is paying attention. No one can hear, obviously.

She stares at the curtain hanging off the rail. In her haste she had pulled it off the rail last night. She studies the pattern on the material, dark blue with orange squares. The revolver man shifts his weight from left to right. He looks up and glances out the window. She wonders whether he really would shoot them, two unarmed females. She studies his profile, his hair, his jacket, his hands. She is surprised that he is so well dressed and wonders whether all bank robbers dress in this way. Or is it a sham? She recalls her grandmother saying that you could always tell a person's class by their shoes. She glances quickly at the revolver man's shoes. They're scratched and in need of repair. Grandmother certainly knew a thing or two.

She wonders what her grandmother would do if she were here: talk them into the ground probably, or take herself off. She recalls the way her grandmother used to come and go, slipping in and out of the spirit world, muttering nonsense about a bear spirit. As a child, Makepeace had accepted her grandmother's vision without question. But as she grew older, she realised that not every one could walk in and out of a person's mind at random.

Ah Makey, you shouldn't ha' shut me out like that. You should ha' trusted me and paid more attention, gal...

Cut it out, Grandmother.

She rejects the featherlike touch of her Grandmother's voice in her mind. No knowing where that could lead. She looks swiftly at the revolver man and forces her thoughts onto something safe: food, toast with honey and eggs, brie and coffee, hot chocolate. Suddenly, she is filled with a desperate desire to eat. She swallows, nervously. The young man shifts restlessly in his chair. 'I gotta eat,' he announces. She looks up hopefully. The young man gets up and leaves the room. She can hear him looking for the kitchen. He returns, disgusted.

'Is there anything to eat in this place?'

Makepeace half-smiles an apology. 'It's Friday today, I usually shop on Saturday morning.'

The young man turns in disgust.

'I can go and get something. It's not far,' she offers. The young man looks at the revolver man. The revolver man looks bored. Makepeace is disappointed. The young man ignores her and goes back to the kitchen.

'There's coffee and tinned milk,' she shouts after him.

Makepeace wonders whether he might make them all a cup of something. The young man returns with a single cup of coffee. He picks up a comic and begins to read. Makepeace draws a deep breath and settles down to wait. She imagines herself a secret Samurai, able to cut down both men with a sword. She takes the fantasy as far as she can in her mind, then begins to feel a wave of self-pity: if only she hadn't opened the door in the first place.

Makey you gotta stop dreaming and do something, gal. Otherwise they'll truss you up like a fat sow and kill you.

Grandmother, what are you doing?

I'm telling you to stop wandering off.

You're a fine one to talk.

I'm an old lady. Old ladies get to do what they like.

Like hell.

Watch your manners.

I'm sorry.

That's better.

I thought you were dead, anyway.

Of course, I'm dead.

Makepeace feels a sudden wave of grief.

Now stop fretting.

I'm sorry.

That's the second time you've said that.

I'm s –

Makey

Grandmother, you can't keep popping in and out of my head or I'll go crazy, as you did. And I don't want to. I don't want to. I want to be like everybody else.

You're not like everybody else.

I can pretend to be.

When will you learn to use what you have. Instead of hiding it under layers of flesh, or ballet dancing with that Japanese fellow.

Grandmother.

Do it.

'Grandmother.' Makepeace finds herself half-risen from the sofa, staring at the revolver man. She averts her eyes hastily and blushes under the scrutiny of three pairs of eyes staring oddly at her.

'Excuse me.'

She notes how late it has become and wonders how much longer she can stay in control.

Evening begins to cast its shadow. Fatigue has settled down to a dull drowsiness. She finds it difficult to move either arms or legs, as if they've suddenly grown heavier. She thinks: Grandmother's right, they'll shoot me, and I won't even be able to get out of this sofa. She dozes lightly with her eyes open. Odette, she notes, has closed her eyes. The young man has begun to play with a flick-knife, opening and shutting it. He's only a boy, after all, she thinks. He's related to the revolver man in some way, but she can't figure out how. She stares at the poster of the bear and can almost see its paw moving towards the head of the young man. She feels an enormous amount of pity for her captors and wonders where it has come from.

Suddenly, the revolver man looks at his watch.

'It's time,' he says.

She opens her eyes. She seems to be staring out from behind layers of flesh and muscle as if she has, somehow, grown in size.

The young man is eager to get going. 'What about these two?' he asks. She holds her breath.

The revolver man speaks. 'Tie them up.'

The young man disappears, returning with a couple of belts. Makepeace begins to tremble. The young man is going to tie her up. She can wait patiently all night if necessary but she cannot, will not, be tied up. The young man approaches. She cringes inwardly.

'Don't touch me!' she says, her voice rising in panic. She lumbers up from the sofa.

The young man stops at the sudden resistance. Makepeace is a broad, big-boned woman, of indefinable race. All he needs to do is tie her arms, and if he has to rough her up, so much the worse. He is in a hurry to leave. He puts his hand on her arm.

'I said not to touch me!'

He grips her arm. She sees red. The muscles in her neck bulge.

'GRRRRRRRR!' she growls. Her movements are slow, clumsy.

'GRRRRRRR!' She takes the young man by his arm. He screams. Her totem is a bear. She is a bear. She hugs him in a grip so tight he almost faints. The revolver man aims his gun at both of them.

'Uncle Jack!' screams the young man. The revolver man hesitates. Makepeace tosses the boy like a toy at the revolver man and they both fall to the floor. She lurches to their side in one leap and holds one head, the blond one, as if she will snap it off with her fingers.

Makepeace!

Grandmother.

That's enough.

The transformation evaporates. Makepeace eyes the two men with a mixture of curiosity and embarrassment: they were related. She turns to Odette. Odette is staring oddly at her.

'Wow, that's some brown belt,' says Odette, moving away gingerly.

PERFECT SECRETARIAL COLLEGE

Li li scurried past the reception, her bag full of shopping. Once in her room she bolted the door and sat down breathless. She felt sick: sick from flu and fever. Once she had recovered from the climb up the stairs, she began unpacking her bag: tins of fruit, sardines, packets of instant noodles and aspirin. She fumbled for the orange juice. Damn. She'd forgotten it. She would have to go out again. She wondered whether she would be able to manage that. Take a rest, then go out. She stared at the food on the table: at least there would be enough to eat over the long weekend. She hated weekends, especially the bank holiday ones; nothing to do except sit in her room. She never went out. She had given that up months ago. Nowhere to go and people always stared because she was alone.

'What's a nice oriental girl doing here on her own? Why don't you come and...' She shut the thought out quickly. Yes, she hated weekends. She preferred weekdays; at least she had classes to go to. Perfect Secretarial College; she was going to be a 'perfect secretary'. No point coming all this way to end up an 'imperfect secretary'. Her parents had done their best. They had paid the fees and the flight. Secretary wasn't as good as doctor, but she could still earn more than most people when she got back home.

Li li sat on the bed and surveyed the room. She had lived there now for eight months and it had taken her all that time to get used to it, to having a room of her own when she had always shared with her sisters. The room was dingy and gave her the feeling of being crowded in: a bed, a table, a wardrobe and already it was crowded. She had cut out old magazine pictures and stuck them on the wall but they only served to underline the dinginess.

Li li sat on the bed and stared at the pictures: one was of a basket of oranges and reminded her of the fruit back home. She sighed and wished she could go back home to normality, instead of this dingy room and these ghost people. If she was back home she would be chattering to her sisters, or going for a stroll in the warm evening, or having something to eat. Li li hugged herself and began rocking backwards and forwards on the bed.

In the first few months she hadn't got to know anyone, not a single person. They were all distant ghost-people in the student residence, or at the college, and try as she might, she could not get them to pronounce her name properly They called her Lily, instead of Li li. Everyone came to study and then went away to their family and friends.

At the School for Perfect Secretaries, they had suggested that she take extra English classes. There was no point in being a perfect secretary if her English wasn't up to scratch. She had enrolled at the International School, joining the large classes where the student teachers practised. These classes were cheaper than the 'proper' ones. She had sat through a series of bad lessons and then got into the swing of it, doing her best to help out the student teachers. The practice class was where she had met the Blond Giant, a cheerful, good-looking boy from Rio. He was studying to be a doctor. He had sat next to her one day and been her partner for the conversation drill.

'Would you please open the door.'

'No, I'm sorry my hands are full.'

He had laughed as if to say, The English are so dull or their language is anyway.

During the break, the Blond Giant had continued the conversation.

'Where do you come from?'

Li li wondered if he was still practising his sentences. The Blond Giant smiled. Li li decided it didn't matter.

'I come from Taiwan.'

72

The Blond Giant smiled again, a warm golden smile. 'A beautiful island.'

Li li was speechless with joy. He knew her country. She didn't have to explain where it was. Li li blushed, the pink tinge spreading over her round face.

Li li got up from the bed. The evening had begun to cast its shadows: wardrobe shadow, table shadow, bed-head shadow. She switched on the light. It cast a yellow hue and made the room look even drabber but at least the shadows disappeared. Outside, the traffic noise had dwindled from a steady flow to an occasional hum. The rush hour was over. She wondered whether to go out once more for the orange juice. One more effort, then she wouldn't have to step out into the ghost world. She would disappear, or it would cease to exist until Tuesday. Li li licked her lips. She was thirsty. Her thirst reminded her of the orange juice. She put on her coat and unbolted the door.

The street was dark and full of city noises. She shivered. The dark wasn't friendly as it was back home. It was cold. She walked past the restaurants. Some of them were already crowded. If only she were brave enough to go in and order a meal. She felt an acute aching, as if by sheer longing she could be part of it all. She walked on towards the shopping square.

The supermarket was crowded with Friday night shoppers. She walked past the tinned fruit, Weetabix, frozen peas, around the edges avoiding the people in the centre aisles. The bright lights and the crowd made her feel queasy, as if she was looking through the glass of a goldfish bowl. She purchased two cartons of orange juice and more aspirin to be on the safe side. She walked home.

She thought of the Blond Giant. Where was he? A feeling of longing possessed her. She hadn't seen him for two weeks.

Li li sat on the bed and stared at the pictures. She thought of home again. The disgrace. How could she go home a perfect secretary – with a big belly?

She felt sick. Sick of the ghost people and the worrying and the longing and the loneliness. If only she hadn't come to this strange, cold country. She hugged herself. Her life was full of if onlys: if only she was different; if only she wasn't so shy; if only she was beautiful and blond and smiling and perfect like the heroines in the storybooks back home. If she had blue eyes and blond hair or even green eyes and brown hair, the Blond Giant would marry her and take her to Rio. She would make a good doctor's wife. She would have the... the baby, a son perhaps, and maybe she would visit home now and again.

Li li clutched her belly, 'Aiee-ya, Zhemma ban, zhemma ban!' She thought about the weekend. Long weekend. Long enough to disappear and be sick and be better. Yes be better. No more sickness. If only she didn't feel sick all the time, then she could think, think more clearly what to do.

She got up from the bed and found her satchel. She took out two bottles and placed them on the table: one brown, one clear. She found the carton of orange juice and placed it beside the bottle. She took a glass and placed it beside the orange juice. Where was the Blond Giant, why wasn't he here when she needed him? She poured juice into the glass and waited. There were footsteps in the corridor. Was it the phone? Was it for her? The footsteps stopped near her door.

'Phone call for Room 6.'

She heard the door opposite open and shut, the sound of footsteps padding away She swallowed her disappointment. Ah! she was sick of it. She held up the brown bottle to the light.

'Gangbe!' she said, and drank the contents. Without drawing breath, she downed the orange juice then leaned back gasping for breath. Tears streamed down her face. She wiped them away with a corner of the sheet and reached for the other bottle: folk medicine to start pain, aspirin to dull pain. She took six with one gulp of orange juice. Surprising how good she was at swallowing tablets. She kicked off her shoes, took off her skirt and edged her way into bed. She would take the rest later. It wouldn't take long, not long. The best thing would be to sleep through it and afterwards the sickness would disappear. No more sickness; she was looking forward to that.

The pain in her stomach woke her – a terrible searing pain that ate away at her insides. She began to shiver. Cramps. She clutched her belly and willed the pain away. It went away but then came back in waves, each wave making her tense every muscle and hold her breath. Ayee! Was she going to die? She wanted to vomit. She switched on the light and lay there panting It will pass. It will pass. She peered at the clock – only eleven thirty.

The next wave sent a hot trickle down her legs. Blood. She was bleeding. Nothing to worry about. Only a period. She got out of bed. Must not get blood on sheets. She hunted around for sanitary napkins. Only two in the packet. She placed one between her thighs but the blood soaked through straight away. She replaced it with the other one. She needed to go to the bathroom but that meant getting up and going along the corridor. Sink. She dragged a chair to the sink and peed in there. The oozing between her legs continued. She wondered vaguely what to do and almost dozed off.

The next spasm caught her by surprise and made her fall sideways off the sink, banging her elbow. Ayee, how long did it take? She took a towel and stuffed it between her legs. She would have to wash everything before taking it to the laundrette. She crouched on the floor waiting for the next spasm. The pain was so intense it made her bowel move. Ayee-ya! Now from both holes. Tears streaked down her face. She began to tremble. So much mess and now it was on the carpet. She cleaned herself, wrapping two towels between her legs. More aspirin for the pain. She took six more aspirin. The bleeding continued. So much blood. Too much blood. She was bleeding to death. She must get help. She stumbled to the door and stopped. The door was the last barrier. She thought of the ghost people, the old man at the reception desk. No. Too much shame. It will get better. It will pass. Better to sleep. She crept back to bed and laid down exhausted.

She woke again, her eyes wide open, staring at the ceiling. The ceiling was slowly getting lower and lower. It would suffocate her. She tried to move but her body was pinned to the bed, like a trapped insect, she thought. No strength, no strength to get up. Trapped on the bed... Must stay awake otherwise the ceiling... Help me! The ceiling is falling in.

Her mouth moved, uttering soundless words. Trapped in a

nightmare with a falling ceiling. This is only a dream; you will wake up soon. Li li looked at the ceiling helplessly. It was so low it almost touched her nose. She could not breathe, she would suffocate. She struggled; and in her last attempt to resist, the ceiling became a bird, an enormous plucked chicken.

'Ai-ya, help me, help me!'

Li Li lay on the bed raining sweat, locked in a delirium. Is this what she came for? To die in a foreign land. She drifted off.

She woke again. This time because of the wetness. The whole bed was wet. So much blood. She panicked. How was she going to get the bed clean? She tried to rise but felt too weak. She turned on her side and tried to vomit on the floor. Nothing but a little yellow liquid streaked with blood. She turned on her back and drifted off. At least the cramps had stopped.

On Tuesday morning Mrs. O'Brian knocked on the door of number five. There was no reply. She knocked again to make sure. Balancing the sheets on one arm, she reached for her bunch of keys. Tuesday mornings were the worst.

They'd all be getting over the weekend and everywhere would be filthy. Students! They'd no idea how to clean up after themselves. All she was supposed to do was hoover up and change the sheets. No one mentioned the filth after the weekends; cigarette ends, vomit and worse; a person never knew. Still, at least this one was tidy.

The smell made Mrs. O'Brian pause before opening the door. God help us. Not this one as well... She stood in the doorway, staring at the mess: blood, vomit, sheets, and black hair lying under... She turned abruptly and fled down the stairs to reception. My God, this was too much. She reported number five to reception, delivered the rest of the sheets and went home.

'I knew as soon as I turned the key,' she said to her husband. 'They couldn't expect me to clean that mess up even if they paid extra. And she was such a nice girl. Oriental. So quiet, God help us. I expect it got too much for her.'

SHORT FUSE

She always approached the house from the left. If she came from the right, she had to pass the dog. She and the dog were enemies. It is possible that her neighbour, Mr. Phillips, was the real enemy, but it was the dog that growled, so she hated the dog – a brown bull terrier with a long face. Every day on her return from work, the dog would wait for her. If she approached from the right, passing directly in front of number 24, the dog would bark wildly and shake the gate. If she approached from the left, it would simply growl. The ritual was always the same. She would be carrying a bag of shopping and some extra sewing; the dog would growl or bark, following her progress from the other side of the railings. When she got to the door, she would fumble with the key, balancing the shopping against her legs. She would open the door and let herself in. The dog would stop. It occurred to Gladys that the dog directed most of its venom at her and her family, rather than the other six or seven residents of the house. This filled her with a quiet fury that belied the outward show of resignation.

Once inside the house, Gladys would climb the stairs to the second floor where she and her sons occupied a room with a small kitchen. The room was divided into two: the 'bedroom' – three single beds, a chest of drawers, an old wardrobe; and the 'living room' – a table, three chairs, a settee and an armchair. The effect was an overcrowded feeling that made the occupants permanently shrink inwards.

One day, Gladys, returning from work, forgot to approach home from the left. It was a Friday. In the pocket of her mustard-coloured coat was an envelope with her wages. On her left arm was the sewing to be done at home; on her right arm, a carrier bag full of shopping. In the bag was the reason for her forgetfulness: a yellow mango, lying like a precious egg on a nest of shopping. The mango had cost her four shillings in a shop along Westbourne Grove and she had already promised herself the sweetest part – the seed. Pleased with her purchase, she had carried on walking, forgetting to turn left so she could pass around the square.

She arrived at her house, eager to be out of the cold and thinking about the tasks to be done over the weekend. The sight of her near the gate set the dog off barking. Gladys stood still, caught like a trespasser. The dog hurled itself at the gate in a volley of barking. The gate sprang open and Gladys' nightmare began. Attracted by the fur in Gladys' workbag, the dog opened its jaws and attached its teeth firmly to the bag. Gladys, seeing her livelihood under attack (each fur coat cost £300), and feeling that her person would be the next target, dropped her shopping and set about hollering. The whole street came to a standstill. Passers-by stood and gaped; residents peered out of windows. Some of them had to stifle a desire to laugh at what they saw: a middle-aged Chinese woman in an ill-fitting coat, locked in combat with a brown bull terrier. At the woman's feet was a broken carrier bag, its contents on the pavement. In the gutter lay a yellow mango, misshapen through its fall from the bag. No one moved to help.

Gladys' son, Gary, alerted by the sound of shouting in the street, ran downstairs. He could not detach the dog from Gladys, nor Gladys from the dog. Suddenly, Mr. Phillips appeared and, moving with a speed surprising for someone so bulky, prized open the dog's jaws, took it by the collar and dragged it inside without a word of apology. Gladys stood clutching her work bag. The shouting had made her hoarse and now the sudden disappearance of the dog had rendered her speechless. She gathered her dignity around her, re-arranging her coat, pushing back her hair. Yet she made no move to go in, even when the shopping was collected. As she stood on the pavement, five years of exile caught up with her. She shook with anger and fright.

'Come inside,' Gary pleaded.

She allowed herself to be led inside.

From that day on, a kind of craziness entered Gladys, a slow rage that burned on a long fuse to the dynamite. Perhaps the rage had been there all along, coiling itself around in layers. From the first week in Inverness Terrace, when the landlady lifted the lids of her cooking pot to peer inside, Gladys was aware of hostility. She knew the look that said: no coloureds, no children, no animals, and bore each insult, each act of hostility, as a mark of her exile. Until the dog. The dog lit the fuse to her rage.

The night the dog attacked Gladys, she dreamed of home. She knew it was home, because it was hot and her hair was sticking to the back of her neck. In her dream, she is walking down a street looking for someone. Her mother. She passes a house and comes across a pair of shoes tapping. The shoes are tapping out a rhythm. She carries on walking down the street and comes across her backyard. The yard is full of fruit trees but without fruit, except one tree with a yellow misshapen mango. She stretches out her hand to pick the mango and hears a growl. Her blood turns cold: the only dog that can climb and it has climbed over the wall to her. She panics. The dog will surely bite off her leg. She makes a dash for the latrine, runs inside and shuts the door.

She can hear the dog scratching on the wooden door, scratch, scratch, scratch. The sound fills her with loathing. Suddenly, she recalls that she is at home, in her own backyard. No dog is going to attack her in her own yard and get away with it. She sees an old broom and grabs it. She opens the door ready to beat the dog. But there is no dog. Only Mr. Phillips. Broad, bald Mr. Phillips, with the pink, baby cheeks. He looks at her and through her. She raises the broom to strike.

Before she can strike, she wakes in front of her cooking pot. She has fallen asleep while cooking. Taking a peep under the lid, she discovers that the food has not been cooking at all. The gas has gone out. She fumbles around and finds a shilling to feed the meter. But the gas ring still refuses to work. Suddenly, the landlady is standing in front of the pot, a look of disapproval on her face. It is she who has switched it off at the mains because she will not tolerate the smell of Gladys' food. Gladys must stop cooking this sort of food or leave.

She drifts between waking and sleeping. Sidney, her husband, stands by her bed looking down.

'What you doing here?' she says, without words.

'I come to tek you home.'

She is supremely happy, but she cannot get up from the bed. Her eyelids are too heavy. Try as she might, she cannot get off the bed to start stitching the coats. If she can stitch enough coats, she will be able to go home. She longs to go home. She should never have left.

She opens her eyes and in the dim light sees the shape of her youngest son, Delbert, lying in bed. Her eyes follow the shape of the bed, the table, the room with the cold corners. Saturday. She can afford to lie in bed longer, but refuses to. There are too many things to do and she is anxious to begin.

This morning she will go to the butcher, because tomorrow, she will make black pudding. The desire for black pudding has arisen out of her dream of back home. Lying under the blankets, she traces her dream backwards to the point at which she hears the dog growling.

Mentally, she adjusts the dream and gives the dog a thrashing. Satisfied with this, she slides out of bed and lights the gas fire. Quickly, she slips on girdle, stockings, blouse, cardigan and a skirt. She goes to the kitchen, has a wash, and combs her hair. Next, she boils water to make tea. As she reaches for the tea bags, she sees two tiny black droppings.

'Now we gat mice!' she says, in despair.

She sweeps up the droppings and cleans all the surfaces carefully In the meantime, Gary joins her in the kitchen. The kitchen becomes crowded and each carries out their task with as little movement as possible.

She busies herself preparing breakfast and lunch.

'Two bread is enough or you want three?'

'Two is enough.' Gary says.

She butters the bread generously and puts ham on each slice. She cuts the sandwiches in two and puts them in a box.

'If you gat a chance you must see if you can get some rat poison for me.'

Gary nods. He seldom speaks. The burden of being in some way responsible for his mother and his brother has made him silent. Other boys, in the same year at school, interpret his silence as passivity, or cowardliness and avoid him. He has learnt not to mind. He eats his breakfast, puts on his jacket, and leaves for his Saturday job. The morning is cold but there is something he likes about the quiet streets.

At home, Gladys has decided to scrub the floor to rid it of any hint of mice. As she scrubs, she recalls snatches of her dream, like the memory of something unpleasant. Since the dog attack, a plan has been forming in her head. The plan is so devious she is not even aware of it herself. She only knows that she must get herself and her sons home within the year, whatever the government, or the situation back there. As if to confirm this, she imagines her home in Subryanville, the wooden floors, the long windows, the frangipani tree. As she cleans the floor of the kitchen, she mentally dusts the corners of her home, throwing back the jalousies to let the light in.

By the time she has finished cleaning and given her son Delbert his breakfast, she is ready to face the butcher. She would prefer to stay in and send Delbert who, at ten, is capable of shopping and actually seems to enjoy it. However, she cannot load him with her responsibility, she must deal with the butcher herself. Before putting on her coat, she goes to the kitchen window and peers out. The window looks out into the concrete yard where the dog exercises. She hopes the dog has been taken out for its daily walk, but is disappointed to see it chasing its tail aimlessly. Gladys is filled with rage. She grabs the bucket of water she has used to clean the floor and hovers by the window ready to throw it. Suddenly, she is overcome by fear: fear of the landlady, the other residents, and the knowledge that she will have to find somewhere else to live. Above and apart from this, she is afraid of Mr. Phillips. Mr. Phillips has never directly addressed her, but she knows all that she needs to know, from his stare. Surprised by her fear, she puts the bucket down and goes to get her coat.

That evening Gary returns to find her stitching. Each coat she stitches earns her extra overtime. The more money she earns, the closer she feels to home. This is part of the plan. She stitches each lining with precision, each stitch being exactly the same. When Gary enters the room she looks up.

'It still out?' she asks.

Gary nods. There is only one 'it' that his mother refers to: the dog. It dominates their comings and goings. Gladys tucks the last stitch in the coat and puts it aside. She goes to the kitchen to check on the food. The food is ready.

'You get the poison?' she asks from the kitchen.

Gary pulls a packet from his pocket and hands it to her. From his other pocket he pulls out an envelope with ten shillings in it. He puts that in a jar on the mantelpiece. The thought that he might hold back some of his wages does not occur to him. The money he earns is a part of their survival.

In the kitchen, Gladys puts away the packet. Tonight she will lay small quantities of poison to see if she can stop what might be an invasion of mice. She waits until Delbert returns from his bath upstairs before she begins to dish out the dinner. On his return, she looks at him critically. His crew-cut hair and dimples make him attractive.

'I hope you wash behind your ears.'

Delbert turns an ear for her to inspect. She smiles and sets out the plates.

On Sunday, Gladys prepares to cook black pudding. She does not cook it early in the morning for fear that the smell will penetrate the other rooms and return with a complaint from the landlady. Instead, she waits until lunch time. She hopes the smell of garlic, blood and herbs will mingle with the smell of the other residents' cooking. As she prepares the runners in which to stuff the mixture of rice, blood and herbs, she hears the dog barking wildly down below. Is a coloured person coming into the house and he pass in front the gate, she thinks. Five minutes later, there is a knock on the door. Gary answers the door and a smile lights up his face. Gladys appears at the kitchen doorway and she too smiles, the first real smile for weeks.

'Harold!'

A tall Chinese man and a slender ten-year-old girl enter the room. The man takes off his hat as he enters. Gladys wipes her hands and rushes forward to hug her younger brother and his daughter.

'Y'all muss'e smell the black pudding! How is Olive and the other children. I see this one getting big.' She helps her brother off with his coat, all the time talking.

'The dog bark you, nah?'

Harold nods.

'I gon kill it one o' these days!'

'Why you don't move, Glad? You and that dog and this place. You can't even get mail here without that woman opening it.'

Gladys sucks her teeth. 'Me gon move again! Is four times I move already. If I move is home I going.' She hangs the overcoat on the front of the wardrobe. 'Gary, bring uncle a drink. You want sweet drink or tea?'

Harold shakes his head, 'Don't trouble yourself.'

'Trouble! Is trouble when you come all the way from Turnpike Lane to see we. What you want? Tea? Coffee? You must stay and eat with us.'

'Make it a coffee then.'

'Gary, bring uncle a coffee and a sweet drink for Jeanie.' She turns to her niece. 'She get big, like Delbert. You want to watch television, Jeanie?'

Jeanie nods.

'Delbert, turn on the television.'

Delbert obediently turns on the television in the 'bedroom'. The picture is fuzzy, but good enough to pick out Shirley Temple, dancing.

Gladys joins her brother, sitting down in the arm chair. She stares affectionately at him, noting his horn-rimmed spectacles and his hair greying at the temples. Harold pulls out an air mail envelope from his jacket and hands it to her.

'Sidney write,' he says.

Gladys takes the letter eagerly, and puts on her spectacles to read it. She reads the letter from her husband quickly, and as she does, a look of disappointment crosses her face.

Harold tries to make himself comfortable, but the settee is too low for his legs and he succeeds only in looking awkward.

'I hear things bad over there,' he says.

Gladys nods.

'Sidney coming over this year?'

Gladys takes off her spectacles. 'He ain' say. He might come for good the way things stay.'

Harold half smiles, half shrugs. 'Might be for the best.'

Gladys stares at the letter. 'I di' plan to go home next year.'

Harold shakes his head. 'The old BG done. Better to stay here. I getting citizenship for Olive and the children. You should do the same, Glad.'

Gladys shakes her head. She never intended to stay and still does not.

Harold and his daughter spend the afternoon with them and then leave at 4.00 o'clock, carrying a parcel of black pudding. As he puts on his overcoat, Harold says, 'You must let me know if you want to move and I will come.'

Gladys nods. She knows her brother would help her move if she asked, but she knows that she will not ask: he is struggling on the brink himself.

Later that evening, with the television buzzing in the 'bedroom', Gladys reads her husband's letter again. She shakes her head at the part that talks of a bloodbath.

'Black against East Indian and we Chiney in between. Gawd. Things proper bad.' She bows her head in defeat. 'An I di' think I going home!'

Later still that evening, Gladys packs away the black pudding. Carefully, she wraps each black sausage in grease-proof paper and puts them in the 'refrigerator', outside the window. As she puts the last parcel on the window ledge, she peers down and sees the dog with its nose pressed against the gate. Chia! In this country, even the dog more important than we.

She sends a thought of pure hate to the dog. Tonight, she is on a short fuse. She wonders what she will do now that her plan to go home has been shattered. Perhaps she should take her brother's advice and move. Perhaps she should get a place closer to him. She is filled with despair at the thought of moving, of packing everything again, facing people's stares; the look that tells her all she needs to know about white and coloured. *I bin live here two years and now I gat to move because of a dog.* She surveys the kitchen, her eyes unable to focus, her mind wandering around in circles. Suddenly, she remembers the invasion of mice. She must do something about it.

Silently, she goes to the window and retrieves one of the parcels of black pudding from the ledge. She unwraps it and takes out a sausage which she begins to open. She takes the packet Gary handed her the previous evening and pours the content into the sausage. She can hear the music Gary is listening to on the radio. 'She loves you yeah yeah yeah. She loves you yeah yeah yeah...'

Gawd. That is the kind of music they listening to now. She reties the sausage and places it on the window ledge. The thought occurs to her that Delbert might see it and eat it. She shudders. Suddenly, the black pudding, once innocent, is now deadly. She retrieves the sausage and ties it with string, knotting each end with the precision of a seamstress. She hangs the sausage outside the window, ready. Tomorrow she will look for somewhere else to live.

Slowly, she has a wash and prepares for bed. Before she retires, she makes one last check on the dog. She can see its shape in the dwindling light. Calmly, she takes her sewing scissors and opens the window. *A dog is only a big mouse,* she reasons, and snips at the string. The sausage falls into the yard below.

She walked swiftly up the street, past the seedy hotels, through the passageway and on to the estate. The night was damp. As she passed the steps leading down to the courtyard of the first block, she saw a scuffle between two men. She averted her eyes and hurried on.

As she approached her block, the tension inside her increased: women were not safe on the estate. She forced herself to walk the last fifty yards to her block and then bolted up the steps. She stopped, out of breath, in front of the flat and fumbled for her keys. At last. She let herself in. Relief. The two pimps had unnerved her.

She hung up her coat and went to the bedroom to check on Joe. The door was still tied with a scarf to stop him from leaving his room if he woke. She knew she shouldn't leave him like that, but she did anyway. She hadn't found a sitter yet and she had decided to go out on the spur of the moment. She untied the scarf and poked her head around the door: Joe was asleep with his rabbit tossed to one side. She breathed a sigh of relief and went back to the sitting room.

She finished her cigarette and tried to make herself comfortable in the armchair but the money in her pocket kept pressing into her leg. She took it out, stared at the four tens and two fives and then stuffed them carefully down the arm of the chair. Today had been a lucky day and with any more luck she would soon be able to buy a three-piece suite. With any luck. Perhaps she relied too much on luck, but then, what else was there to rely on? She switched on the television, watched the European Figure Skating Championship for a while and then went to bed. The day had been exhausting but at least it hadn't been boring.

Joe woke her up the next day by crawling into her bed. She gave him a hug, tickled him for a bit and then told him she needed to sleep some more. Joe pressed his face close to hers and said:

'Is it Saturday today, Mum?'

She opened her eyes and stared solemnly at him, 'Yes, all day.'

'You said you'd take me to the zoo on Saturday,' Joe said.

She groaned. 'So I did. But not so early in the morning, eh. Go and play for a bit and let Mum sleep.' She turned over and pulled the covers up. Joe crept out of bed, played with the tassel on the bedspread for a while and then disappeared into his own room. She fell asleep and woke again at 8.00. Joe had turned the television on and was playing with the volume. She got out of bed, told Joe to stop messing around and went for a wash. They had breakfast together watching 'Motormouth'.

As she spooned cereal into her mouth, she made a mental note of all the things she had to do. She liked Saturdays because they were different: mapped out; plenty of things for her and Joe to do; not like at the hotel where each day merged into the next and worst of all there was never any privacy. Now she and Joe could do what they liked, when they liked. All she needed was someone to talk to, another adult. Then it would be perfect. She thought of Sandra. Had she moved from the hotel? She felt loneliness creeping around the edges of her well-ordered day: evenings were the worst, when Joe was in bed.

She cleared the breakfast things and began to gather the laundry. She stuffed it into a black bag and put it together with the Daz by the door. She checked Joe's room to make sure he hadn't wet the bed or stuffed his socks under the mattress. Satisfied that Joe seemed to have gotten over his bed-wetting, she gathered everything together and sat down again to put on her make-up: a touch of mascara around the eyes and some pale lipstick, just in case. Just in case of what she never knew, but she felt safer with her face on, ready to face the world. She took the black bag and opened the door. Joe carried the Daz as together they left for the laundrette. At the bottom of the stairs, she saw one of her neighbours, Pat, a short stout woman in her late forties. Pat had been friendly when she had first come to see the flat, even inviting her in for a cup of tea. It was only after she had seen Joe that Pat had become distant, hostile even. Joe was a beautiful enough child: curly black hair and brown eyes. It was his colour that Pat objected to: Joe was a definite, though indescribable shade of brown. Hazel nodded briefly at Pat and passed on. She didn't want to be rude, but she didn't want to be friendly either. A week ago someone had scrawled 'nigger lover' on the wall by the bins. Hazel suspected Pat's teenage sons, but she wasn't sure. In any case, she didn't care. If they couldn't accept Joe, then she couldn't accept them. She recalled her mother's reaction when she first saw Joe at the hospital: disbelief and then embarrassment. How could her daughter produce a coloured child? Sometimes Hazel wished she too was coloured. It might have been easier for Joe. Joe's father was an American; his ship had docked in Bristol. Where was he now?

The sight of Joe making a trail with the Daz brought her back to the present.

'Joe! That's naughty now!' She grabbed the Daz and marched on to the laundrette. They were early enough to get a machine straightaway. She put everything in to wash and then left for the sweet shop to buy a newspaper. Joe had to have a packet of sweets and she a bar of chocolate. She felt resigned about the chocolate: she had already put on half a stone since the move and looked set to put on another half. She sat in the laundrette eating and reading while Joe played with an empty carton.

'Eh luv, mind what yer doing.' Hazel glanced up to see Joe falling over a basket of washing.

'Joe! That's enough, come and sit down. D'you want to go to the zoo this afternoon or don't you?' Joe looked as if he might rebel, but then he smiled sheepishly and came and sat beside her. As she waited for the clothes to dry she studied herself in the glass: blond hair, long angular face. She wasn't pretty but there was something attractive about her face. Long ago, when she left school, she had wanted to be a model. The nearest she had got to that was selling clothes in 'Top Shop'. God, life was a joke.

After the laundrette, she made some sandwiches and she and Joe set out for the zoo. They went there so regularly she had bought herself a zoo pass. In the last frantic week before the move, she had tried to buy every thing she would need because she had promised herself she would come off the street. She hadn't realised how much she would need to make the flat decent: carpets, curtains, somewhere to sit, a fridge. She had slid back into a trick or two, promising herself that once she had the settee that would be it. Last night she had finally got the money for the settee. But there was still Joe's birthday and clothes and shoes so he could start off school looking decent. How much longer was she going to...

'Mum! Look at that!' Joe was pointing to a chimpanzee swinging with a baby at her stomach. She smiled. 'That's like me and you, Joe.' Joe seemed intrigued by the thought. He stood and watched the monkey for a while, then dragged her over to the penguins.

At six o'clock it was time to leave. For some reason she left through the North Exit and made her way to the bus stop as if she were going to her old place, the hotel. She thought of Sandra. Sandra was only a short bus ride away. She felt a sudden longing. She turned to Joe. 'Shall we go and see Sandra and Christie, Joe?'

Joe looked lost, as if he couldn't remember who Sandra and Christie were.

'You remember, Christie, don't you? You used to play with her.'

Joe nodded.

'Do you fancy seeing Christie?'

Joe nodded again. That was settled then. She was going to see Sandra.

'Look, Mum, there's a bus!' said Joe, waving wildly. The bus pulled up alongside but Hazel hesitated.

'Aren't we getting on, Mum?' said Joe, anxiously.

'No. Let's wait for the next one, son,' she said. The bus driver shook his head and shut the door.

She had missed Sandra more than she cared to admit. But Sandra was the past. Besides, they had gotten too close. She retreated from the thought. The barrier came down.

'Mum, look another bus!' shouted Joe.

'That's a number thirty, son, see if you can see a two and a seven, twenty-seven,' she said.

That was it. Finally she had admitted it. She and Sandra had been close, too close. That had happened over the summer. Joe and Christie had been taken out for the day by the council play workers. She and Sandra had remained in the hotel doing their hair and nails. They had both had a shower and were feeling cool and relaxed. Sandra had done her nails for her and that had brought them close. Sandra had caressed her arm, then her legs and the passion had flowed. Sandra's skin was sweet and golden brown like honey. Her smell was – Hazel could not describe Sandra's smell; it was like the essence of Sandra. She smiled at the thought. She should have bottled it and called it 'Essence of Sandra'. She had never felt passion before; men rarely turned her on. She opened her legs. It was her job. Sandra was different. She had loved her all summer and that loving had scared her.

When she got her letter from the council she was over the moon. She showed the letter to Sandra and waited for her to be excited. But Sandra wasn't; there was an unspoken agreement between them that when either of them left the hotel, they would leave for good. Their passion was a summer thing, their friendship, a result of being confined in the hotel. Besides, each wanted different things. Sandra wanted easy money and an easy life. Hazel wanted more. She wanted to 'settle down' and earn good money, legit. She wanted to 'do' something with her life. She had told Sandra all this from the beginning. Sandra had laughed, veiled her eyes with her long lashes and continued to caress her.

'Two – and sev– en, twenty-seven, Mum, look!' cried Joe.

Hazel patted Joe's head affectionately 'So it is. Well done, Joe!'

She looked at the bus and shivered with nervousness. Yes, that was it really. She wanted more than anything to come off the street, be legitimate, respectable. Sandra could never offer her that. She stood, confused. Sandra was Sandra and the old life was the street. Was it the street that she hated or Sandra? She recalled Sandra's smell: 'Essence of Sandra'. No. She could never hate Sandra; run away from her, perhaps, but not hate. She considered the past few months. Her entire life had been empty. She had simply gone through the motions of living.

The bus pulled up alongside and the door opened. She waited for Joe to jump on and climbed in after.

When they got to the hotel they found Veronica, the manageress, at the desk.

'Hi stranger. How are you? How's the new flat?'

'Hi Veronica. How are things?'

Veronica groaned. 'Same as usual. Eh, hasn't he got tall?'

She chatted to Veronica, noting the dingy wallpaper and the smell of cooking. How different her life was now. She was glad she had left.

'Is Sandra around?' she asked, carefully.

Veronica shook her head. 'She left a month ago.'

Hazel stared at Veronica blankly. 'Left?'

'Yep. Just like you.'

'Do you know where she went?'

'No. Didn't leave an address. Most people don't.'

'Did she get rehoused?'

'I suppose so.'

Hazel tried to hide her disappointment. Sandra had gone without leaving an address. It wasn't any different from what she herself had done. She bit her lip. She supposed it served her right. She turned to leave.

'Aren't we going to see Christie, Mum?' Joe asked, anxiously.

'No, Christie and Sandra have moved, like us,' she said.

'Hang on, I could have sworn there was a letter for you. Came a couple of weeks ago,' Veronica said, fumbling among the piles of paper on the desk. Hazel waited patiently. Veronica handed her a small square envelope. Hazel put it in her pocket.

'Thanks a lot. Bye.'

She read the letter at the bus stop several times.

Hampton Estate, No 29. It's a dump.

S

Hazel smiled. Then she began to laugh: Sandra knew her better than she knew herself, it seemed. She put the letter away and stuck out her hand to stop the bus.

Depression. She could feel it coming over her. Like a cold sea mist it hovered and then settled into her very being, the moment she knew that Remi was leaving.

Remi said, 'I'm moving out.' But it didn't seem right; they had been living together for two years; a person didn't get up and go like that.

'I've been living too long in your shadow. I need more space,' she said. And it was true: the flat was too small. As for her shadow, she felt guilty. It was her fault.

Madelaine sat in the corner of the living room watching Remi pack. Remi was precise: folding everything, neatly, before putting it in her case. The way she was leaving was precise too: no tears or tantrums, just, 'I'm going to move out.'

The spring sunshine poured through the window exposing the fact that the bookshelf was empty, She's leaving, Madelaine thought. If I don't say something, she'll really go. What shall I say? How did we get into such knots?

'We need to talk this over. You can't leave like this.'

Remi paused for a second. 'It's your flat. I should be the one to go.'

'You're avoiding the issue. I don't want you to go. There's no need for it.'

Remi pushed her dark fringe from her eyes and looked at Madelaine. 'I want to go,' she said simply.

Madelaine felt the pain cut through her. Remi wanted to go. She bit her lip.

'Do you want me to give you a hand with your stuff?'

'Only if you want to.'

Madelaine nodded. 'You've found somewhere, then?'

'Yes. In Stoke Newington, with a friend of Iffy's called Judith and another woman, Sharon. It's short-life,' she added. 'There's no bathroom.'

Madelaine thought, Iffy again. I hate Iffy. She said, 'You can take the iron and the saucepans and the rice cooker if you like.'

Remi looked up. 'Thanks. I think Judith has loads of stuff, otherwise I can get some.'

Madelaine withdrew. She floated up to the ceiling and out of the window. Camberwell is one hell of a noisy place. A shithole really. Why on earth do I live here? Why don't I live on an island somewhere, miles away from anywhere?

'Do you mind if I move tonight?' said Remi.

Madelaine hovered in and out of the window. Who me? Mind? She settled back into her corner. 'No, It'll only take about two trips in the car.'

'Thanks.'

Keep your thanks. You've betrayed me and I don't want to see you again.

When Madelaine got back to the flat she was exhausted. I hate Sunday evenings, she thought venomously. She reached for the telephone. Come on, Deborah, answer the phone. She let it ring. Nothing. She went to the bathroom, washed her hands and carefully removed her contact lenses. She peered at herself in the mirror. Your nose is too long. She shook her head; the beads made a clicking noise. Time to get rid of these locks, my girl. Altogether too much hair and, besides, Remi said she liked it. Madelaine banged her fist on the wall. Fuck Remi! She made a blind swipe at the wall again and sent a bottle of almond oil flying. I hate Remi and I hate Iffy and that whole house.

'I need space,' she mimicked, 'Space to fuck Iffy'. Madelaine gave a cry and sent the rest of the bottles flying.

'I'll never live with a lover again. They come in here, take up your space and, just when you get used to them, they move out!'

Madelaine marched into the sitting room. She peered at the clock. It was 8.30 pm; only 8.30! She tried ringing Deborah again. No reply She let the phone ring out of spite. Why aren't you in tonight, Deborah? She put the receiver back and dialled her mother's number.

'Hello, Mum?'

'Yes.'

'Madelaine here.'

'Yes, Madelaine.'

'You okay?'

'Yes, I'm fine.'

'Everyone okay?'

'Yes. What about you?'

'I'm okay' Pause. 'Remi's moving out.'

Silence.

'Why she moving out?'

'Flat's too small.'

There was a grunt.

'Okay, Mum, I'll come and see ya next week. You got any of that saltfish?'

'I'll get some.'

'Great. Bye.'

'Bye.'

Click.

Madelaine checked the clock. It was 8.45pm. She rolled a spliff, making sure all the tobacco stayed inside the paper. She struck up and inhaled deeply. Relax. Don't panic. She watched the smoke coil round slowly and then allowed herself to think, cautiously, about Remi.

It was exciting at the beginning, especially when they found out that they both came from the same small island. Hell, it was a small world. Remi didn't know anything about Trinidad, being only two when she left. Madelaine had been five, not really old enough either. It hadn't mattered though; what memory lacked, imagination made up for; and there had always been her parents.

Madelaine shuddered at the thought of her family. When Remi had moved in, Clive had said, 'Why you living with that coolie girl?' That had been the end of any sisterly affection.

My brother, your head is a bag of wind. 'You're nothing but a fart,' she had said. And from then on she had kept a distance between them.

Only her mother was allowed to meet Remi and that had been under very controlled circumstances. Afterwards her mother had said, 'She dress up like a boy'. Then she had added, grudgingly, 'But I suppose it better than all that make-up they wearing now.'

From then on Remi was accepted, or tolerated, Madelaine wasn't sure which. She squirmed and shook out the thought. She allowed herself once more to think, carefully, about Remi. She loved Remi. She loved her body. Slim and snug and dark. Darker than hers. She smelled of sweat and ashes of rose. Madelaine groaned. She had finished the spliff and she was still wide awake. She reached for the telephone again and dialled Deborah's number.

'Hello.' (At last) 'Is Debbie there? It's Madelaine.'

'No, she's out.'

'Oh.'

Silence.

'Are you all right?'

Madelaine tried to stop the tears. No I'm not all right; my lover's left me. 'Yeah. I'm okay. Bye.'

Click.

She rolled herself another joint.

The weeks passed quickly for Madelaine. She kept busy by making sure she was out every day and every evening in a kind of frenzy. She saw friends she hadn't seen for months, avoiding anywhere she might see Remi. Weekends were the most tricky: Saturday night and Sunday evenings. Loneliness always threatened to creep up. She saw a lot of her mother, driving up to North London most weekends.

Hardly anyone rang to speak to Remi, so she supposed everyone knew. She wondered what they thought. She knew Remi's family would be pleased. They hadn't liked the idea of her moving in in the first place.

It wasn't until the last bank holiday in May that Madelaine found herself with nothing to do. She wasn't sure how it happened. She had been so busy going to meetings and getting her work ready for the art exhibition, the bank holiday had crept up and caught her by surprise. She telephoned Deborah at the last minute only to find that she had gone away with Sheila. This is where you find out how many friends you haven't got. They're all around jostling to see you, then suddenly they disappear at Christmas and bank holidays. Huh!

Madelaine paced around the flat. I wish Remi was here. Why don't you phone Remi!

The phone rang. Madelaine picked it up, eagerly. 'Hello!'

'Madelaine?'

Disappointment. 'Yes?'

'Allison here. We're off to Suffolk. Do you want to come?'

Madelaine hesitated a second. Suffolk. She had promised about a year ago not to put herself through the Suffolk routine again. Ever since those white people had stared her out of the Rose & Crown. Allison had supported her, but then Allison was white and that was the trouble with the country: all green and white and not a Black face anywhere.

'Are you still there?' came Allison's voice.

Madelaine glanced around the four walls in the living room. 'Yeah, I'm still here. I'd love to come.'

'Great! We'll pick you up at 2.00.'

Click.

Suffolk was a mistake. Allison and Siobian had only invited her out of pity and when she withdrew, they couldn't deal with the silence. They had wanted a comedian. Instead, they'd got a dull, silent woman aching for Remi, aching so deeply it was a wonder they hadn't felt it.

They drove back to London in silence: Allison, Kit and Siobian.

'We won't come in,' said Allison, dropping her off at Camberwell.

Madelaine got out of the car, relieved. 'Bye now. Thanks for the weekend.' Polite to the end Madelaine.

She ran up the stairs two at a time, having the absurd feeling that Remi was waiting for her. She opened the door, expectantly. The flat was quiet. And empty. Madelaine slumped down in the armchair. I can't stand this emptiness. I can't stand it. What am I going to do? She drew herself inwards.

When Remi had first moved in they had talked about this: the dreaded parting of the ways. They had decided in their dewy-eyed way that, somehow, they would deal with it when it arose (if ever). Madelaine sighed bitterly. When Remi had first moved in, she had not been in London long; no job, no prospects and her parents furious with her for dropping out of University. She had needed Madelaine and Madelaine had responded by becoming her lover, friend, family. A mistake, she thought. But she had needed Remi too; she had needed her steadiness, her dependency, her availableness.

'Come back, Remi. I need you. I promise I won't take you for granted again.'

Madelaine reached for the phone. There was no phone in Stoke Newington. Shit. I'll call Iffy. Even Iffy will do. She dialled Iffy's number.

'Hello?'

Madelaine put down the receiver. At least she had some pride left, thank God. It was the only thing that kept her going. Otherwise she would fall to bits. Or fling herself into the river. She glanced around the empty room. There was life before Remi, and there would be life again, she thought grimly. 'Come on, girl, pull yourself together. There's loads of work to do.' She went to the drawing board and got out her pencils. She took a clean sheet of A4 and started to draw a cartoon. My lover's gone and I don't know why. Maybe the flat was too small, maybe we got to know each other too quickly, maybe we didn't get to know each other at all.

Madelaine screwed up the paper and threw it at the window.

I do know why: she did all the home-caring and I did the creating. I got into my work because I wanted to be famous. I wanted to see my name on books: illustrations by Madelaine Pearce. Madelaine banged her fist on the desk and sent the pencils flying. It was my friends and my work and she organised herself around me. Until she got involved in that policing group and met Iffy. Yuk! I hate Iffy And now she's gone, I don't want anything but her.

Madelaine took another sheet of paper and began to draw again. How did we get into such knots? It was my friends, my work and she slotted in. I was strong and she was dependent. Dependence = weakness. I hate weakness. Hold on, Madelaine, this is right off. It's true though. I didn't like it, but it suited me. Until she started wanting things for herself and I got jealous. I can't stand her needing other people.

Madelaine got up from the desk in disgust. I need you Remi! I really do. I can't think. I can't work. And I hate myself. She looked wildly around the room. Remi, I need to talk to you. Phone me, damn you!

The telephone rang. Madelaine looked at it fearfully. Slowly, she picked up the receiver. 'Hello?'

'Madelaine?'

Silence.

'It's Remi.'

'I know'

'Our phone's been connected now.'

'Yeah?'

'You been busy?'

'No.'

'Can I see you some time?'

Yes anytime. Now. Immediately. 'Yeah sure.'

'When?'

'Tomorrow.'

'Sounds okay.'

'No, on second thoughts, how about now?' Pause. 'I missed you.'

'Shall I come round to the flat?'

'No. I'll come to you.'

'Okay. Give me half an hour.'

Madelaine looked at her watch. 'I'll come over at 4.00?'

'Fine. See you then.'

Madelaine put the receiver down. I'll come to you on your terms. Because what we had... Correction. What we have is good. None of that fly by night stuff. Perhaps we can begin to unravel the knots.

The sea mist parted and drifted upwards. Madelaine began to hum.

HOMECOMING

Margret held her breath as the plane landed at Penang Airport. Her face, expressionless in the white light, masked a flood of confusing emotions: joy, anxiety, fear. She had made this trip home many times and each time the joy of seeing the familiar landscape had crowded out any misgivings she had about returning. This was home, even though she had long ago ceased to belong.

Margret sighed and turned to her companion. 'This is Penang.'

Her companion nodded. 'I'll be glad to get out of this awful seat and stretch my legs. Now I know what you mean about the journey It's too long.'

Margret gathered up her things and waited for a gap in the line of passengers slowly disembarking.

'You've forgotten your glasses,' said Jack.

Margret took the glasses gratefully. She was glad that Jack was with her. Jack would remind her of who she was in the coming tangle of family relationships.

'I'll meet you in front of the customs desk,' said Margret as they arrived in the hall. The two women separated to have their passports inspected.

'How long do you plan to stay?'

Jack flushed. 'Three weeks,' she said clearly. The official glanced at her and stamped three months in her passport. Jack passed through to the customs desk.

'They're in a good mood this evening,' she said, as she met up with Margret. 'I guess we have an easier time though,' she added.

The two women walked into the waiting area together: one tall and thin with close-cropped hair; the other, slightly shorter with black, shoulder-length hair. Several people glanced curiously at them.

'I guess I'd better get used to being stared at,' said Jack, dumping her case on the floor.

'Yeah, it'll make a change.'

'Phew! It's hot.'

'This isn't hot yet,' said Margret, cheerfully. She glanced quickly at the groups of people waiting. Her parents were late.

Margret began to worry at the thought of meeting her parents. She squirmed at all the questions she knew Jack would be asked. 'What do you do?' 'Where do you live?' 'How old?' She wondered why her parents bothered to ask anything at all. The end result was always the same. Jack would be seen as one of her peculiar English friends, and possibly the person from whom she had learnt that 'Western' habit of independence. Margret forced her thoughts back to the present.

'Look, there they are,' she said, pointing in the direction of a group of people. And group it was, for they had all come to meet her: parents, brothers, sister-in-law, children.

'Margret!'

'How!'

'Good to see you!'

'You lost weight.'

'Had a good trip?' The two women were enveloped in a warmth of family greetings.

'Goodness me, you've grown in the last two years,' said Margret, hugging her niece. Then she turned and looked at Jack. 'Everybody, this is Jack!'

'Jack is a boy's name-lah,' said Margret's nephew. Margret ignored him. She wasn't about to offer an explanation.

'Come, let's go to the car,' said Margret's father. They went to the car park, her nephews and nieces running ahead, excitedly. She had to get in the car and shut the door before they would stop chattering.

Outside the night was warm and friendly. Penang at it's best, thought Margret. It's good to be home.

She watched the scenery slide past: coconut trees, wooden houses, lights dotted here and there. It was familiar.

'What do you do in England, Jack?' asked her mother. Margret giggled: her mother hadn't wasted any time.

'Bit of this and that,' said Jack. Mrs. Chung looked confused.

'I take photographs mainly,' added Jack.

'Oh photographer!' said Mrs. Chung, smiling.

'I'm glad that's over!' said Jack, closing the bedroom door. 'I was beginning to feel like a gorilla at the zoo.'

'I'm sorry, we went straight in at the deep end, didn't we? I forgot everyone would want to come and meet us.'

'They can't get used to my name, can they?' said Jack, flopping onto the bed.

'Or your hair. Why is her hair so short-lah?' The two women laughed.

'Hey, are we going to sleep this far apart?' said Jack eyeing the two single beds.

Margret sighed. 'No, give me a hand to move the table.'

'Why can't women lovers sleep together,' said Jack, pushing the beds closer.

'Because they're not supposed to be lovers,' said Margret.

'I don't agree!' Jack laughed, and kissed Margret on the mouth.

'Listen, I think we should lock the door,' said Margret.

'I've locked it, already,' Jack replied.

'Why do you move the table-lah?' inquired Margret's mother the following day

'Because it's in the way,' said Margret, looking up from the newspaper.

'You can put your things on it!' insisted Mrs. Chung.

'In the way-lah,' said Margret, firmly 'And anyway, we want to sleep closer!' Mrs. Chung shook her head and went into the kitchen.

'That was bold of you,' said Jack. Margret pulled a face. She wished she could tell her mother why she wanted to sleep nearer to Jack. Perhaps this time she would. Margret shifted uneasily in her chair. She had brought friends home before but this was the first time she had brought a lover with her. Somehow, the thought made her feel vulnerable. Margret pushed the news-paper away and got up from the table.

'Do you want to go swimming today?'

'I'd love to,' said Jack. 'I'm so hot I don't know what to do with myself.'

Margret laughed. 'Swimming will cool us down and then we can go and try the food at the Padang.'

'Now you're talking,' said Jack, perking up at the thought of food. 'Do you think three weeks is long enough to try everything?'

Margret laughed. 'If we eat every two hours, we should manage it.' Jack grinned.

'Food is the thing I miss most when I'm away. I wish I could transport the food stalls in the Padang when I go back.'

'And the sea and the sun,' Jack added.

During the next few days, Margret found herself relaxing into being at home. Everyday, she took Jack swimming or sightseeing. She introduced her to different 'exotic' fruits and even took her to see where she had gone to school as a child.

In the evenings she went shopping with her parents, took Jack to the night market, or visited her brothers. As far as her family went, everyone seemed on their best behaviour. They welcomed Jack, didn't ask any personal questions and always spoke English. It's because I haven't seen them for so long, thought Margret.

Towards the end of the first week, however, she found the equilibrium slipping: she had begun to argue more with her parents.

'I don't want to visit second Auntie's god-daughter and her husband. I don't know them,' she insisted.

'Doesn't matter,' said Mr. Chung. 'You can tell them what you do all this time in England.'

'But I don't want to be shown off to your friends,' said Margret.

'Not show off-lah,' said Mrs. Chung. 'They want to meet you.'

Margret started to protest, then thought better of it. It would only lead to a bitter argument and, anyway, wasn't it all part of coming home?

There were many things that Margret liked about being home. She liked going for walks in the evening and feeling the warm sea breeze on her face. She liked the coconut trees on the skyline and the campong, the toc-toc man on his bike selling food and the short quick showers to keep cool. It all added up to something that took her back to her childhood, something she could call home even though it had long ago ceased to be somewhere she belonged.

'This place has gone down the drain,' she said to Jack one day after finishing a plate of mee goren. 'The portions are smaller!'

'Things change,' said Jack, philosophically.

I suppose they do, thought Margret sadly. She watched the families eating the dip-dip and satay. They seemed the same, only not so many as in the old days. I suppose they've gone somewhere else to eat hot dogs and cakes, she thought. She wondered why she felt so bitter. After all, hadn't she left as well?

Towards the end of the three weeks, Margret found herself arguing not only with her parents, but with Jack as well. They had gone out for a stroll by the sea wall and had ended up arguing over what they would eat.

'All I said was I didn't want anything greasy today. There's a difference between greasy and tasty.'

'Our food's not greasy. What about all those chips you eat?'

'They're greasy! And sometimes, I can eat them and some-times, I can't. What's the matter with you, Margret?'

'It's no good, I feel under too much pressure. I keep arguing with people and I can't help it.'

'Yeah, maybe it was a stupid idea for me to come in the first place.'

'No it's not,' said Margret. 'I wanted them to meet you. I wanted you to meet my mother and I wanted her to like you.'

'That's a big want, Margret.'

'I know I think I forgot how hard it is to be with my parents. They treat me just like they did when I was ten. And damn, if I don't react in the same way.'

'I've noticed you regressing.'

'Thanks!' Margret got up and walked along the sea wall.

'I didn't realise how hard it would be bringing you here. It's like two sides of me coming together and they don't fit. I get so frustrated I spend the time eating or arguing. It's painful.'

'Then why come?' asked Jack, softly. Margret sat on the sea wall and stared out at the horizon. The sea was dark-blue, calm.

'I want to see my parents,' she began. 'My mother really; I'd like to be able to talk to her, tell her what I really feel and care about. It's been sixteen years since I left and although I've been back, I've never really talked to her. I want to tell her about my life. Tell her about you. But I can't. Every time I see her, I keep my distance and we talk about safe things.'

'What did you expect to happen this time?'

'I thought if you were here, it would be easier to tell her I was a lesbian.'

Jack remained silent.

Margret continued, 'But I can't do it; somehow, the time's never right and when it is, something just holds me back.'

'Fear.'

Margret smiled. 'I suppose so. I think I'm afraid she'll fall apart or reject me.'

'She's probably stronger than you think.'

'I'm sure she is,' said Margret. 'Sometimes, I panic and wonder what would happen if she died suddenly. I think I'd be eaten up with regret. I think about this, and then I decide to tell her. But I never do.'

'I think you should tell her,' said Jack.

'You can talk,' said Margret, angrily. 'There's Lesbian Line, and Gay Liberation back there in England. Here it's different. You go to school and then to work, if you can find any, and then you get married and that's it. And if you're a lesbian, tough. Keep it to yourself, or throw yourself in the well. There's no such thing. There isn't even a word for it!'

'I'm sorry,' said Jack.

'My mother is old-fashioned Chinese, and the world has to behave in a certain way,' said Margret, bitterly.

'But your mother isn't stupid,' said Jack. 'And I bet she knows about us anyway.'

'I expect she does. As long as you don't put a name to it.'

'It's not the name so much,' said Jack. 'It's the fact that people don't want to recognise our relationship for what it is. So you have to make them. You have to say, look I'm a lesbian, and that's why I'm never going to get married.'

'I don't care about "people". It's my mother I want to tell. I don't want to have this barrier between us all the time. I thought it would be easy to tell her with you here, but it's not, it's worse.' Margret lapsed into silence. She felt tired and dispirited. The whole holiday had been difficult, and she wasn't any closer to her mother now than at the beginning.

She got up from the wall. 'We'd better go eat. It's late and you still have to pack.' She ruffled Jack's hair. 'Let's try the soup.'

She lay in bed watching the light slowly creep into her room. Today was the last day of the holiday and she felt no nearer talking to her mother. Jack had returned home five days ago and she had spent the remaining time with her family. She recalled saying goodbye to Jack at the airport, her head full of unfinished conversations. She had deliberately kept quiet. It would all have to wait until she got back.

I'm the world's best postponer, she thought. Then she remembered her mother. Today she would say goodbye to her mother, without having told her a thing. Margret got out of bed. She walked to the dressing table and looked in the mirror.

'Ma, I'm a lesbian, what do you think of that?' she said, and pulled a face. 'Margret, you're pathetic. You've had three weeks with Jack and five days on your own to tell her.' Margret turned away in disgust. Maybe I should come to terms with the fact that I can't tell her, she thought, glumly.

'Have some more to eat,' said Mrs Chung.

'No, I'll be fed on the plane,' said Margret, looking at her mother. 'Are you sure Pa knows where to meet us?'

'I said "Restaurant" to him,' replied Mrs Chung. Margret

looked anxiously at the entrance. 'Be sure to eat, and get plenty of exercise,' continued Mrs Chung.

'I'll try,' said Margret.

'Jack will meet you at the airport?'

'Yes, Ma. Don't worry.'

'She a good girl, Jack.'

'Woman, Ma.'

'Girl when you my age,' said Mrs Chung cheerfully. 'Get on well with her, huh?'

'Yes,' said Margret. She took a deep breath and continued, 'We're thinking of living together after I get back.'

Mrs Chung raised a thin, pencilled eyebrow 'Early days! Maybe you still courting-lah.'

Margret threw a quick look at her mother. Either she'd got the wrong word in English, or she knew. Margret felt a sudden rush of embarrassment. It spread out over her cheeks. It's me that can't handle it.

She looked at her mother's round face and then at her hair. It's getting grey at the roots because she's stopped dying it. Margret was shocked. She's getting older.

'Yes, we'll talk about it first,' said Margret finally 'But I'd really like to.' The two women looked at each other in silence. Margret was the first to look away.

'Come, here's your father,' said Mrs Chung. 'Time to go.'

The two women made their way to the departure gate.

'Take good care.'

'And you, Ma.'

'Dress warmly.'

'I will.'

'And write more often.'

'I will!'

GOODNIGHT, ALICE

She drove all the way along the coast from Oakland to Santa Cruz and when she got there she stopped at the Boardwalk and bought herself a hot dog. It was early. There was plenty of time to relax and then go and register. She saw a couple of women with spiky hair, maybe gays, maybe going to the retreat. She ignored them in case they weren't.

She thought once more about the weekend and considered going home again – back to Kay. She'd never been to anything like this before. And never again, please god. Hell. All the bitching and politicking. What am I doin' here?

She turned and wandered into the arcade. If she left straight away, maybe she could catch Kay before she left. Maybe they could make a weekend of it in Sacramento, Labour weekend after all. She looked at her watch. Kay would already have left.

She found herself in front of a game machine and automatically began to feed it with money Racing was her passion – anything from cars to bikes to horses. 49, 48, 47, 46, 45 Blip! How could she miss? 43, 42, 41, 40 Blip! She grabbed the wheel grimly She was loosing her grip. 39, 38, 37, 36, 35. That's better.

She emerged from the Boardwalk an hour later. Glancing once at the sea, she strode to the car. She might as well get it over and done with. She drove slowly up to the University. Asian Pacific Lesbian Retreat. Huh! How many Asians were there going to be? Maybe ten or eleven, all blind as bats and spouting rubbish.

The road curved up to the University and afforded her a view of the sea.

'My god this place is like a holiday camp! Don't tell me

people actually study here with all those trees and this scenery.'

She saw the sign APL and turned left. Asian Pacific Lesbian. Huh! This had better be good.

Women. All shapes, sizes.

Don't let it get to your head, Al. Take it easy. Walk slowly to the registration desk and take the stupid grin off your face. You're cool.

'Hi, are you registered yet?'

She looks down at a pair of horn-rimmed glasses.

'No, er, I wasn't sure I could make it.'

'Glad you made it. Did you hit a lot of traffic?'

'Sort of.'

'Haven't I seen you around before?'

'Rapture maybe, or did you ever try for a loan at the Western Fed? I work there.'

The woman laughs. 'No I didn't. Rapture I guess. What's your name?'

'Alice. Alice Lee.'

'Mine's Julie. You can fill in the form and pay over there. I'll just make you a badge while you're doin' that.'

'Thanks.'

She moves along to another face with spiky hair and sunglasses.

'Hi, you staying for the whole thing?'

Nope. I'm outa here as soon as you can say, kiss my –

'Maybe.'

'Okay, fine. Sort out the accommodation over there.' She turns to another desk and steps back in astonishment. Christ!

'Fraid you'll have to share. It's all twin-bedded rooms.'

Alice stares at the woman. 'Really? Can I share with you?'

The woman smiles. 'I already have a room mate. But I'm on the same floor. Here's your keys.'

Alice grins and takes the keys. If they're all like you, honey, I'm staying.

The woman adds, 'You'd better go eat right now. Dinner finishes at 7.00.'

'Thanks! Thanks a lot.'

She follows a couple of women to the dining room. The noise hits her as soon as she opens the door. Holy Jane Ann! Look at all those dykes: Filipinos, Japanese, Indian as well. Not a white woman in sight. And all looking so intense. Ha! Maybe it was a good thing I came without Kay. Not that she coulda come.

'Hi, Alice!'

'Gracie!' She put the tray down and gives Gracie a hug.

'Easy honey, I might like it! What brings you here anyway? Thought this was too intellectual for you?'

She shrugs. 'Maybe.'

'Whatcha doin these days. Hiding out at Oakland?'

She grins. 'Maybe.'

'How's Kay?'

'She's gone to Sacramento for the weekend.'

'So you're free.'

'Maybe.'

'Look, is that all you can say? I expect at least a one line answer after ten months?'

'Come and eat with me.'

Gracie laughs.

Later that evening Alice walks to the car and collects her case. That wasn't too bad. Gawd, I didn't realise I hadn't seen Gracie in ten months. Must be the married life. She recalls the time when she used to nod at Gracie at Anna's night spot. Gracie had been the only other Asian gay around. Must have been all of – fifteen years ago!

She slams shut the trunk and makes her way towards the dormitories. As she rides the elevator to the fourth floor, she stares critically at her reflection in the mirror. Alice, you're getting crow's feet around your eyes and your jacket's looking a bit, well, old. One thing I hate is a dyke in old leather. Huh! Let me see room 412, 405, 403, 401. Oops, wrong way.

She hesitates in front of 412. Here I am at the screwball retreat. Might as well have fun while I'm here. I've never been with an Asian before. I wonder what they're like in bed?

As she puts the key in the door someone opens it from the inside.

'Oops, excuse me.'

'S'okay. Hi, I'm Alice, your room mate. You're –?'

The woman smiles and backs away. 'Jeanie.'

Alice walks forward. 'Good ta meet you, Jeanie. Lemme see now, do you snore?'

Jeanie smiles. 'I don't think so.'

'Good. I'm a light sleeper.'

Alice dumps her bag on the chair, pokes around the room and decides it will do.

'Single beds and a desk each. Christ, these students have fun. Oh and a lamp!'

Jeanie laughs. She fiddles around awkwardly in the wardrobe then goes back and flops on the bed.

'Whew, I'm beat and I haven't done anything yet.'

Alice's turn to smile. 'Wait till after the Social on Saturday night and see how you feel.' She opens her bag and starts unpacking.

'Where are you from, Jeanie?'

'New York.'

'That's a long way to come for a retreat.'

'I guess.'

'How did you know about it?'

'May Young told me about it last year. She's on the planning group. I came with her and her girl friend, Kit. I've been looking forward to it all year and now I'm here, I can't believe it. How about you?'

Alice looks up from her unpacking. She decides not to mention Kay to her new room-mate yet.

'Oh, someone told me and I figured I'd check it out. I live in Oakland so it wasn't far.'

'You must know a lot of the women here.'

'No, I don't.'

'How come?'

'Don't get around much.'

'Funny, I thought if I lived here I'd go to everything. I mean look at all the women.'

'Yeah, now that *is* a surprise.'

There's a knock on the door. 'Come in!'

Two women enter.

'You coming down for the plenary, Jeanie?'

'Yeah, sure. Alice, this is Kit and Gail.' Alice looks up to see the woman from the accommodation table. She goes into her routine: an admiring look, followed by a swift grin, then rapid conversation. 'Hi, you gave me a good room and a great room-mate. What more do I need?'

Gail laughs. 'You're easy to please, right?'

'That's me. Say, are you next door?'

'No, I'm along the corridor, number 405.'

'I'm on the right floor anyway,' says Alice, cheerfully.

Jeanie puts on her sweater and turns to Alice. 'You coming down now?'

'Sure.'

Alice leaves the room last so she can check herself in the mirror. Tall. Short hair, round chalky face, leather jacket. Looking good. Good looking.

She sits at the back of the lecture hall with Gail and Jeanie.

'I want to say this is a fine coming together. There's plenty of workshops. And space for more if you want to suggest one. Everything will take place in this part of the campus, apart from eating and sleeping.'

God this is boring.

'And also I wanna say how pleased I am to be here and to see so many Asian faces. I lived in a place where there was only me and well, me. I never dreamed I'd sit in a room with more than a hundred like me. Even if I don't go to anything else, I feel positive.'

Cut the crap.

Later that night, Alice lies in bed, staring at the ceiling. Suddenly, Jeanie's voice comes out of the dark. 'What did you think of the plenary, Alice?'

'Okay. A bit boring, but okay.'

'What did you expect?'

'I'm not sure. I've never been to anything like this before. I'm not political and I don't talk much.'

'Being a gay is political, isn't it?

'No it's not. It's different, but it ain't political.'

'Why did you come then?'

'Dunno really. Someone, Kay actually, told me about it. I saw the stuff and decided to come.'

'Something must have attracted you.'

'Yeah, the women.'

'You're on the cruise for women?' says Jeanie, indignantly.

'Sure.'

'Wouldn't you be better off in the bars?'

'More choice here.'

'You might be wasting your time.'

Alice turns over and nestles down snugly. 'I don't think so. I bet most of the women here are on the make. Why else would they come? I know they spout this stuff about coming together and moving forward. But I bet, underneath, they're eyeing each other up to see who they can score with.'

'You're joking!'

'No. Okay, that's too crude. They're on the look out.'

'Are you on the look out?'

'Yes and no. I'm married see. To Kay. But there's no harm in looking.'

'Alice, you're weird.'

'No more than you, honey. Why did you come then?'

'I came to meet other women. Share experience. Talk about what it's like being a gay in New York. A Chinese gay who doesn't fit in. I grew up in Delaware with no other Asians around. I want to talk about it. Talk about being part Filipino. Why I hate my father. Why I can't talk to my mom. How hard it is to find other Asians.'

'Kid, you need a shrink for all that, not a retreat.'

Jeanie laughs. 'Maybe.'

There's a long silence.

'Don't you have anything you wanna talk about, Alice?'

'Nope.'

'Are you happy with who you are?'

'Yep.'

'I envy you.'

'Know something, Jeanie?'

'What?'

'You think too much.'

'Goodnight, Alice.'

'G'nite, Jeanie.'

Alice sleeps in the next morning well up to 11.00 o'clock. She manages to make the second round of workshops and chooses the one on 'safer sex'. Her attention is caught but she comes out not having contributed to any of the discussion. She meets Jeanie on the stairs.

'Hi, Alice. You woke up at last. What did you think of the workshop?'

'Okay I guess. A bit big, but interesting.'

'I thought it was fun, but I guess we always laugh about sex to cover the embarrassment.'

'Yeah, I didn't realise other people did that tongue thing too.'

They both start laughing.

'Say, do you want to come swimming this afternoon?'

'No. I want to go to the adoption workshop.'

Alice shakes her head. 'I say this for you, kid, you got stamina.'

'Not really. How many times in my life do I get to sit in a room full of Asian Pacific lesbians?'

Alice shrugs. 'Once a year if it keeps going, I guess.'

They head for the dining room.

Alice chooses not to disappear after lunch. Instead she goes to another workshop on relationships with white women. She feels personally challenged even though she knows no one in the workshop. She comes out angry and goes off to play tennis with Gracie. She lets off steam in the changing rooms.

'You know some of those women have a nerve. All of twenty-four and they think they know it all.'

'Yes, O aged one.'

'Come on, Gracie, we're fifteen to twenty years older than some of them. That counts for something.'

'Leave me out, honey, I'm only thirty-seven.'

'That makes you thirteen years older.'

'Yeah, well don't remind me. How come you're so mad anyway?'

'I was mad at that young kid for saying we should only go with Asians.'

Gracie picks up her racket and takes a quick look at herself in the mirror.

'Maybe we should. That at least would cut the crap, and we have enough of it as it is.'

'But what if you don't know any other Asians? What if you don't like any? What if you grew up in a place where you were the only one, and the only other one was so and so's sister and, God, she was ugly?'

Gracie laughs. 'Then you got yourself a problem.'

'All I can say, it was different in those days. You were glad enough to spot another gay of whatever colour. Besides, I never liked a woman because she was gay. I always liked first and found out later.'

'Maybe that's your trouble, Al.'

Alice shakes her head and walks out onto the court. Later that evening, Alice finds Gail sitting on her own outside the Social and manages to talk to her without going into her routine. She discovers that Gail is with Susan but continues anyway.

'Don't you find it a little hard having a relationship with someone in Hawaii?'

'I guess so. I call once a week and so does she. It used to be every day but like, it was costing a fortune. There was the time difference too. They're three hours behind so I'd have to wait until it was cheap time, but late enough for her to get home. Now we save everything for the weekend, but we talk a long time.'

'Why doesn't she come over here?'

'Hawaii is her country. She loves it there. She's in the middle of a degree, anyway, so she'd have to finish that first.'

'Why don't you go over there?'

'She never asked me.'

'Christ!'

'No, it's not true. She did; I guess I'm a little scared of it. Every time I've stayed there for more than a month I get that isolated feeling. She lives in Kilua, you know; it's north of the island. I guess I'm town bred.'

Alice finds herself thinking Susan must be mad. She keeps

her thoughts to herself and stares at Gail's profile in the dark.

'She plans to come over when she's got her degree.'

'Who?' says Alice, absentmindedly.

'Susan. It's only another eight months.'

Meanwhile anything can happen, thinks Alice.

Suddenly, Susan comes walking across the courtyard.

'Gail?' The two women look up. 'I've been looking for you all over.'

'We've been sitting right here. I thought you said meet outside the Social.'

'No. We've been watching slides and having a Lua. I thought you were going to come along.'

Gail springs up and follows Susan. 'I'll see you later, Alice.'

Alice sits and stares into the night. Boy, those two have got trouble. She gets up slowly and walks towards the dining hall where the Social is being held.

The Social turns out to be an anti-climax as far as Alice is concerned, especially since no smoking and no alcohol is allowed. Alice finds it impossible to cruise without a beer can in her hand, so she ends up talking to Jeanie instead.

'You look kinda dreamy and spaced out, kid.'

'I guess it was the workshop this afternoon. It was really emotional.'

'Yeah, well this is the time to relax and forget it.'

Jeanie continues, almost to herself, 'You know this place is like a mirror, you see reflections of yourself all over and some bits you like and some bits you can't stand, and its all kinda shocking.'

'Yeah, and way too deep. This is the Social, remember?'

'Hmmm.'

Alice waves a hand in front of Jeanie's face. 'Anybody home?'

Jeanie laughs, 'When did you come out, Alice?'

'Look, we're not in the workshop now.'

'I know, I just wanted to know. You're so cool and cynical and—'

'If you really want to know, I'm not cool at all and I'm scared shitless of getting old. And if you really want to hear another coming-out story I'll tell you later.'

'Okay, let's dance then.'

Alice stands up. 'Honey, I thought you'd never ask.'

Just as Alice is about to fall asleep that night, Jeanie's voice floats through the dark.

'So when did you come out, Alice?'

'Oh gawd, this woman,' groans Alice.

'You said later.'

'I didn't mean 4 o'clock in the morning.'

Jeanie turns over and pumps her pillow up. 'That's the best time for coming out stories.'

Alice groans again, wrestles with the blanket and gives up in disgust. 'I thought folks didn't use blankets anymore. Okay, lemme see. The first love of my life was Stacey.'

Jeanie nestles down to listen. 'Who was Stacey?'

'Stacey was in 7th grade. But even before that, I think I was always gay. I mean I always liked girls. I was a tomboy myself. I have three brothers and we were always swinging from trees and getting into trouble. I played with the boys but I always liked girls. I liked them soft and pretty because that always made me feel strong. I used to thump them one; that was how I expressed myself. I guess I was awkward as a kid, you know, big and gawky. I didn't fit the Asian stereotype of petite and feminine.'

'So you were aware of a stereotype?'

'Hell, from my own mother. She used to despair over the size of my feet. I'm sure she would have bound them up if she could have.'

'When did you find out you were attracted to women?'

'Well, Dr. Jeanie.'

Jeanie giggles.

'The first girl I fell for was Stacey. She was petite and blond; quiet and sort of timid; although I got the feeling she was no way as timid as me on the inside. I followed her around like a dog and offered her things from my lunch box. She even liked noodles, so I got my mom to put that in all the time. One day she let me carry her books home and I was her servant for life. Her folks thought I was some weird Asian kid their daughter picked off the streets. Or maybe even the errand girl from the grocer shop. I never went inside their house though. I knew my place, see.'

'And what happened?'

'Nothing much. I mooned over her, got passionate, carved a heart on the only tree in our block – Alice and Stacey. Ha! When Stacey got another friend I was jealous. Supremely jealous. I used to take that other kid's coat off the hook and trample all over it. Then I'd hang it up again so there were foot prints up and down. Stacey herself blew hot and cold. Sometimes she'd let me walk home with her, other times, she didn't care for the attention. One day I got in a rage with her and thumped her one. She never told her folks, but she wouldn't talk to me again. Stubborn. But that's what I liked about her.'

'Poor Alice.'

'Poor Alice nothing. I made up for it since.'

Silence.

'Jeanie?'

'Hmmm.'

'Goodnight.'

Both Alice and Jeanie sleep in late the next morning. They get up and struggle to the open forum. By afternoon, they've both had enough and decide to go swimming with Gail and Gracie. It turns out that half the Retreat have the same idea because they meet more and more women on the beach and it becomes a celebration.

Alice looks at the groups of women dotted around her and sighs. 'Say, you know I'm going to miss all this next week.'

'You don't mean to say you like being here with us, Alice,' says Jeanie.

'That's exactly what I do mean. Who else is going to wake me up at 4.00, in the morning, asking for my coming-out story?'

'What about Kay?' says Gracie.

Alice looks suspicious. 'What do you mean, what about Kay?'

'Don't you miss her?'

Alice looks uncomfortable.

Gracie laughs and adjusts her shades. 'It's okay, you don't have to miss her; you don't have to feel guilty either. How long have you been together now?'

'Three and half years.'

'Did she mind you coming away?'

'No. It was she that told me about it. We sort of do our own thing, Kay and me.'

'Modern, huh?'

Alice laughs. 'Maybe.'

They go back to the Campus and spend a quiet evening playing cards and talking. After a few hours everyone disappears and just Jeanie and Alice remain in the room. Jeanie stifles a yawn and deals another round to Alice.

'Do you speak Chinese, Alice?'

Alice barely looks up. Instead she lays down an ace and says, 'There you go again.'

'There I go again what?'

'There you go, asking me all these questions.'

'I'm only asking cos' I don't know you well, and –'

'Yes? And?'

'And you seem to know lots of things.'

Alice throws down her hand of cards and rolls over on her back. 'Come on, do I look like your mother?'

Jeanie starts to laugh. 'Not really.'

Alice continues. 'Let me ask you a few questions for a change.'

Jeanie sits up. 'Okay go ahead.'

Alice collects the cards together slowly, giving herself time to think. 'Okay, er, what you doin' Tuesday night?'

Jeanie laughs.

Alice grins shame-faced. 'Okay no I mean, how old are you Jeanie?'

'What if I said, I'm doing nothing, Alice, just waiting for you. That'd blow you away, wouldn't it?'

'Ah, Jeanie, you know me too well. But I was serious anyway.'

'What – about my age?'

'No about Tuesday night.'

'I'm twenty-three, and Tuesday night I'll be staying at Gale's and flying out Wednesday morning.'

Alice gets up, stretches and gets into bed with her clothes on. 'Good, then you can come and have dinner with me.'

'What about –'

'Kay?'

'No, the Chinese,' says Jeanie. 'Do you speak Chinese?'

'Yes I do; we'll go for a Chinese meal and I'll tell Kay.'

'Yummm, yeah Chinese; it'll be like an antidote for the poison they've been feeding us here.'

'Why did you want to know whether I speak Chinese?'

'Cos I don't and I envy you. I feel less Chinesey, know what I mean?'

Alice begins to laugh, 'Hell, that's the funniest thing I heard all weekend. How can not-speaking Chinese make you less Chinese?'

'That's because you speak it. I don't. And it makes me feel, well, you know, like I'm not Chinese or something. When I first met May Young (you know May Young?), she used to take me to meet her folks and her mom would try to speak to me in Cantonese. I used to get dead embarrassed. I told her I was half Filipino anyway, because I think my dad was. She thought I spoke Tagalog so I lied and said I did. I tried to learn once, but every time I open my mouth to practice every one falls about in hysterics.'

'Yeah, but some people are weird. And you don't need to take any notice of them. Anyway, look how good your English is. I bet you got straight A's.'

Jeanie pulls the cover over her head in disgust. 'That's what white people say to me, Alice.'

'Gee I'm sorry, Jeanie, I only meant I'd be proud if I spoke like you and to hell with all the others. Anyway how can you be less Chinese. There's no such thing along a scale of 10.'

'But, Alice, you do speak like me, and you also speak Chinese, and I'm just telling you how I feel. And that's stupid, especially when I go into a Chinese restaurant and I can't order, and the waiter looks at me like I'm nothing.'

'Didn't your ma speak Chinese?'
'No my mom's white. I was adopted.'
'Oh.'
Silence.
'Jeanie, I'm sorry. For being such a dope.'

The next morning, Alice goes to the last plenary and then packs her car up ready to leave. She hates saying goodbye so she tries to slip away. Gracie spots her and runs over. 'Alice! you're not going without saying good-bye, are you?'

'Er no, I was just packing the car, Gracie.'
'Am I gone get to see that silly grin of yours, sometime?'
'Sure.'
'Why don't you come over and I'll cook you dinner?'
'Sure.'
'How about Friday?'
'Great.'
They hug.
Alice tries to slip away a second time.
'Alice!'
'Gail?'
'I'm having a party on Thursday. Nothing special, maybe some Japanese food. Will you come?'
'Sure.'
'Give me your number and I'll ring you.'
Gawd, these women are fast! Alice takes out her card and scribbles her home number on the back.
'I'll see you Thursday.'
'Sure.'

Slowly, she drove back along the coast to Oakland, her mind caught in images of the Retreat, talking to Gail, dancing with Jeanie, arguing with Gracie in the workshop. She retraced all the conversations in her mind and wondered how she was ever going to be the same again.

Alice, you're being overdramatic. A weekend with a hundred and fifty Asians and you've gone off the rails. So... Anyone would go off the rails with that many women. Asian Pacific, hmmmm.

As she drove along, she glanced at the sea. It was the first time she was really aware of it. She pulled the car over and got out to admire the view. The wind was strong on the cliffs, but instead of making her feel cold, it filled her with energy. She gazed at the sea: sunlight glinting on green crystal. She thought about Jeanie. Jeanie was right about the reflections. She had caught a glimpse of herself reflected in a hundred and fifty women. And she was shocked. Take it easy Alice. You're forty-eight. She laughed. All the more reason for going off the rails.

She thought of Kay. What was she going to tell Kay? Nothing, she supposed. Suddenly, she felt like a bird in a cage with the door open. Was she going to fly out? She opened her arms as if she was about to soar from the cliffs into the sea. 'Alice, my girl, this is just the beginning,' she said, flapping her arms.